ALLIANCE

A Story of the Great Plains

I0548867

Matthew Blaine

MILFORD
HOUSE

an imprint of Sunbury Press, Inc.
Mechanicsburg, PA USA

MILFORD
HOUSE

an imprint of Sunbury Press, Inc.
Mechanicsburg, PA USA

For information about special discounts for bulk purchases, please contact Sunbury Press Orders Dept. at (855) 338-8359 or orders@sunburypress.com.

To request one of our authors for speaking engagements or book signings, please contact Sunbury Press Publicity Dept. at publicity@sunburypress.com.

FIRST MILFORD HOUSE PRESS EDITION: May 2024

Set in Adobe Garamond Pro | Interior design by Crystal Devine | Cover by Lawrence Knorr | Edited by Lawrence Knorr.

Publisher's Cataloging-in-Publication Data
Names: Blaine, Matthew, author.
Title: Allegiance : a story of the Ohio country / Matthew Blaine.
Description: First trade paperback edition. | Mechanicsburg, PA : Milford House Press, 2024.
Summary: Young Barnabas Locke and his Abenaki friend cross the Mississippi onto the Great Plains, rescuing Spanish siblings fleeing a river pirate with a cache of jewels. They summer with an Arapaho band, but a conflict over gold sends them to Santa Fe. Attacked by the cut-throat pirate, they fight through a night of fire and blood for their lives.
Identifiers: ISBN : 979-8-88819-189-7 (paperback).
Subjects: YOUNG ADULT FICTION / Action & Adventure / General | YOUNG ADULT FICTION / Historical / United States / Colonial & Revolutionary Periods | FICTION / Historical / Colonial America & Revolution.

Designed in the USA
0 1 1 2 3 5 8 13 21 34 55

For the Love of Books!

———— ✦ ————

This is in honor of and respect for
all the Native Peoples who appear
on the pages of The Young Frontiersman series,
with particular thanks to the Hinono'eino,
which means "our people" in Arapaho.
I hope I got it right.

CONTENTS

ACKNOWLEDGMENTS

My trusted first readers (beta readers in publishing parlance) volunteered their invaluable time to the attentive reading of the manuscript of this book, as well as the others in the The Young Frontiersman series. Jim Glenn is a retired writer/editor and outdoorsman who taught me not to interrupt the story line with too many words. Denise Glenn is a talented reader, forager, and woodland explorer. She likes horses and enjoys the ones who trot through the pages of the series. My younger brother, Stephen Balchunas, caught inconsistencies and offered keen insights. Stephen has been my partner and video recorder on many Western adventures. My older sister, Alane Balchunas, provided research and necessary secretarial skills and restrained my more fanciful notions. My diner breakfast buddy, Jerry Treon, provided expertise on period firearms. Thanks are due to our waitresses, who kept the coffee flowing. All my readers generously shared their unique perspectives.

INTRODUCTION

THE VILLAIN OF this chapter in the lives of Barnabas Locke and his Abenaki friend Squando is called Joe Fontaine. That character is adapted from the treacherous Samuel Ross Mason, one of the most notorious of the river pirates who preyed on Ohio River commerce in the late 18th century. In tribute, the names of other 19th-century historical figures have been adapted for fictional characters. For example, Young Raven is loosely based on the later historical Arapaho Chief Little Raven, who acted as a peacemaker among his own neighboring Plains tribes. He welcomed white Americans into his Denver tipi during the Colorado Gold Rush. The Utes called Pike's Peak Tava or "Sun" long before it was named for Zebulon Pike or became the magnet for gold-seeking "Fifty-Niners."

Parts of the Great Plains were originally settled by Native American mound builders from the 9th to the 15th centuries. Our heroes engaged in an ambush at such a mound in the preceding story, *Allegiance: A Story of the Ohio Country*, and saw more of them in the early pages of this story. Migrating

1

Native Peoples followed the mound builders. Starting in the late 17th century, French explorers and trappers arrived, lured by the lucrative trade in beaver pelts. St. Louis, which became the "Gateway to the West," was established by the French in 1764, although Spain had acquired the region by a secret treaty signed in 1762. After the transfer of power, the Spanish confirmed French land grants, and Spanish soldiers provided a military presence. In 1782, the year of this story, Spain controlled trade, taxes, and territory west of the Mississippi River. Much of the region passed into American ownership with the Louisiana Purchase of 1803. History is complicated and often confusing.

The legitimate original occupants of the Great Plains and beyond were the numerous native populations. They orchestrated their alliances. The tribes that feature in this story are the Arapaho, Cheyenne, Ute, Kiowa, Comanche, and, on the periphery, the Pueblo peoples around Santa Fe. These are only a handful of distinct peoples with distinct languages who each established their own government, economy, social structure, and cultural norms. They traded, allied, and warred with one another. They were not "savages;" they were individual peoples adapting brilliantly to both the bounty and the extremes of their vast landscape.

In 1739, the brothers Pierre and Paul Mallet were the first French "voyageurs" to arrive on the plaza in Santa Fe, New Mexico. They had lost their trade goods at a river crossing en route but waited for nine months in Santa Fe, only to receive official word from Mexico City denying them permission for future trade. Because Spain refused to permit French access to trade with either native tribes or the Spanish inhabitants of New Mexico, the Santa Fe Trail did not become well-traveled until the years after the Louisiana Purchase.

To learn more about native "hand talk," I consulted the book *Indian Signals and Sign Language* by George Fronval and Daniel Dubois, published in 1978 by Bonanza Books. It contains a wealth of invaluable information and insights on the cultures of the Great Plains peoples.

Alliance: A Story of the Great Plains is third in The Young Frontiersman series. I hope the books encourage readers to learn more about American history from all its differing points of view. As a disclaimer, I identify myself as a "storyteller," not as an expert or historian in any field. Be assured I have done due diligence in seeking authentic sources for information and inspiration.

Matthew Blaine
Storyteller
October 2022

ONE

---◆---

IN GOOD HEALTH

2 April, 1782
Cahokia
Illinois Territory

Dear uncle Edward and aunt Elizabeth,

I take quill in hand to tell you I am in good health. So is Little Bay, tho we have past through trying times since we left you with all good wishs, March last. I travel with our friend Squando. Tell Molly her brother is in good health. We are now in Cahokia, a trading town on the east bank of the Mississippi River. Tomorrow, if the wether bids fair, we cross into Spanish Territory.

I trust you are all in good health in Vermont. Please tell Ned he comes to mind offen, and I miss his cheerful face. Did he propose marage to Miss Lucy Forester yet? She will tire of waiting if not. I wonder if the apple crop was a bumper this past fall. Are you planting the orchard farther up the hill this spring? I miss your pies, aunt Elizabeth, and hope that Sally will be as good a baker as her ma. Word has reached us that Cornwallis was defeated at Yorktown. Looks like young Enoch will not get his wish to be a soldier.

You might of herd the renagade white man Simon Girty has been killed by a Mohawk. That is not so. He lives still, tho much wounded. He has acted the friend to Squando and to me. He saved my life from Wyandot Indians. He made a plan to rescue Squando from the British. They held him on false charges in gaol at Fort Detroit for many weeks. Simon Girty is not the villan claimed by most. Many Indian people in the Ohio Country listened to Squando's visions, but the British wanted him gone. They said his words stir anger amongst the Indians.

Send word, if you can, about the baby born to Molly and Zeke. Does it do well? Have they repaired the barn roof on my Father's farm? Tell Molly Squando has learnt hand talk so he can speak with Indians out on the plains. I wonder what they might think of his visions.

Cahokia has a post office at the new courthouse. Please rite to me in care of Joshua Jones,

Esq., Boat Builder and Land Agent, Cahokia, Illinois Territory. Tell Ned he is the same sergeant we served under whilst inlisted in Whitcomb's Rangers. He put me to work that mostly suited me these past months. Many like him come here to make land deals on behalf of the Army and speculaters.

That is all for now. I will rite again when able. I send well wishes to all.
y'r affectionate nephew Barnabas Locke

Barnabas raised the quill with a deep sigh of relief. It had been a long letter to write, and no doubt he had got some words misspelled, and Ned would laugh. He knew they would all be glad to hear from him at last. He folded the pages and addressed and sealed the letter with a small prayer that it would some day arrive at the Locke Farm. He had already prepared a parcel of presents, but he made no mention of it in his letter lest he jinx delivery.

"Finished?" Mr. Jones had waited patiently while Barnabas wrote at his desk using his valuable paper and ink. He had employed Barnabas over the winter months to serve as scout, hunter and protection for his surveyors sent far into Indian country, both legally south and, on occasion, illegally north of the winding boundary of the Ohio River. Barnabas had scowled over those missions north of the Ohio, but Mr. Jones paid him well, and he could not abide an indoor life.

"You are missing a good opportunity here, Barny. Business in land and shipping is booming and could make you a rich man." Jones had not been happy with Barnabas's decision to go west in company with his "Injun friend." He was careful, however, not to disparage Squando, whom he had not yet met.

Barnabas replied that he needed to post his correspondence and stepped out onto the rough planking. His attention was seized by a striking young woman in a flouncy red skirt and a frilly white shirt under her embroidered shawl. Her slim waist was set off by a tooled leather belt clasped with a large silver buckle. A thick, long braid of glossy black hair hung down her straight back. Pinned to her head, she wore a man's wide-brimmed slouch hat with silver ornaments on the leather band. She appeared to be engaged in a heated exchange with an equally slim young man, looking much the worse for a long night. Is that a lovers' quarrel, Barnabas wondered. He had never seen one on a public street. He was relieved that he had no such entanglements. Their raised voices drifted across the street to his ears. They were arguing in Spanish, and Barnabas recognized only the word *dinero* repeated several times and surmised that their dissent was over money.

As the pair crossed the muddy street, the young lady and Barnabas was sure she was a lady, raised the hem of her red skirt, exposing a pair of supple calf-high leather boots. They passed him by, intent on their argument and waving eloquent hands at each other. At closer range, Barnabas judged the woman as a practical, pretty girl who liked pretty things. He looked after her until the pair disappeared through the doors of a respectable lodging house. He could not have described the young man.

He shook himself out of a reverie and turned in the opposite direction to the post office. After posting his letter and parcel, he turned a street to the livery where his riding horse, Little Bay, and his two pack horses, Patrick and Henry, were stabled. The pack horses had arrived late last summer with Mr. Jones when he departed Fort Pitt for Cahokia.

Jones had obliged Barnabas by selling him on a handshake these two reliable pack animals, named by Barnabas when they were his pack horses on Forbes Road crossing the Allegheny Mountains. In the livery's locked storeroom, he checked over the inventory of gear and goods that he and Squando had acquired for their western travels. In the first light of morning, they would pack the horses before crossing the river.

Mr. Jones had installed the ambitious Frenchman Jean-Pierre Bellevue and his Abenaki wife to oversee his Fort Pitt operations. They were old friends of Barnabas and well-known to Squando. Monsieur Bellevue was an experienced boatman who understood the construction of keelboats. The enterprising Mr. Jones had expanded his business interests into this lucrative new market. All trade goods and settlers were headed down the Ohio River from Fort Pitt, most of them arriving in Cahokia on their way farther west. Raw goods— timber, crops of all kinds, buffalo hides, salt in kegs, furs—were bound south to New Orleans and then on to the European market.

Early in the evening, Squando rode into Cahokia on the plain brown gelding Barnabas had traded a high-stepping horse for last fall. "Have you named him yet, Squando?" Barnabas asked, patting the horse's nose as Squando dismounted.

"You place great store on naming horses, Barny. A name is not given; it is earned. This horse has not yet shown his true self, so how can I give him his true name? He is a good horse and willing."

The friends dined with Mr. Jones in the private rooms of his establishment, served by a cook who looked disapprovingly at the tall, slim Indian at the table. Mr. Jones, despite his reservations, was impressed by the Abenaki's command of language and manners. In fact, he was deeply interested from the commercial angle as Squando demonstrated his new talent for hand talking, a widespread way of communicating among the plains Indians. The conversation drifted to the improving health of Simon Girty, another man Mr. Jones had never met but had heard much about. Jones was secretly amused that Girty had unwittingly provided him with a valuable report through Barnabas's quick thinking. The infamous turncoat was again working for the British Indian Department in Detroit, sporting a red silk bandana to hide the sword wound that had laid open his skull.

Even the birds were not awake when the two friends quietly packed and saddled their stamping horses at the stable. They rode at a quick clip through the dark streets of Cahokia to the designated rendezvous with a flatboat docked at the river bank. To their amazement, lantern light revealed the presence of two passengers sitting with a small crew of men atop the rough cabin. Barnabas identified the young woman as the Spanish girl in the red skirt he had seen with the same dark-haired young dandy who sat beside her.

The captain made no apologies. "They paid in silver, and they don't take up much space. The woman can keep your horses calm, and her brother can help pole us across." Barnabas's quick eyes noted that the belt with the silver buckle had been replaced with a wide sash. "A brother," he thought, "not her beau."

The captain and his three pole setters loaded the four horses onto the front deck, where they were tied facing the squat cabin. None of them offered the usual resistance that horses feel instinctively about crossing water. The young woman stationed herself at the cabin's low entry. She seemed very eager for departure, nervously scanning the river bank. The gangplank was no sooner brought aboard when lantern light on the dark water moved towards them.

"Pirates!" yelled the rudder man atop the cabin. Two rowboats came out of the dark, each with four burly armed men rowing hard. From the bank above, a pair of men on foot appeared, one of them waving a lantern to guide the rowers. The other, a broad-shouldered figure dressed in town clothes and waving a sword like a baton, directed the attack. He was outlined against the rapidly lightening sky. All semblance of stealth had been lost.

"So you thought to run out on me, Della. Slap me in the face and cheat me of my due. Diego, you chiseling little dog, don't play cards when you ain't got the money to pay up." Clearly, this attack was more a personal vendetta than piracy. But piracy made a convenient cover for dead bodies in the water.

The pole setters immediately abandoned the boat. The captain cussed them roundly but stood firm on the cabin roof with the rudder man crouched at his feet. He fired a musket at the starboard side rowboat, flung the gun to the rudder man to reload, and picked up another. Squando retrieved his bow from his saddle and from the cabin roof, loosed arrows with deadly accuracy in rapid succession. Some rowers were struck by bullets or arrows or flying splinters; others dropped their oars to fire back, but the port side boat kept on course. As it bumped against the flatboat, one of its crew flung a grappling hook, fastening the rowboat tight to the pole setters' low walkway. Before the attackers could swarm aboard, Squando leaned over and shot the pirate dead with his primed pistol, discouraging his mates.

At the boarding end of the flatboat, the action was equally intense. The four horses jostled one another in distress, scrabbling for footing on the unsteady deck. The cabin protected them from gunfire from the rowboats, but they were exposed to the men on the bank. The young man swore volubly but ineffectually in Spanish. His sister withdrew a pistol from her sash. As Barnabas fumbled for his pistol, the girl cooly fired hers, then swore bitterly as the bullet struck instead the lantern holder, who had stepped by chance into the path of the bullet aimed at the large man. The lantern holder yelped, and the lantern rolled into the water below with a dying hiss. The large man rushed down the bank, brandishing his sword and shouting for his gang to board the flatboat.

"Kill the others, but don't harm the woman," he bellowed, flashing his sword at Barnabas, who had jumped off the deck to confront him on the shore.

Due to the dampness of the river crossing, Barnabas had failed to prime his pistol, as he remembered too late in bitter chagrin. But his tomahawk was in his hand. He slashed one of the mooring lines. Before he could sever the second line, the large man with the sword was nearly upon him. "Cut the mooring line with the axe," Barnabas screamed into the face of the frozen Spanish youth looming above him.

He swung his tomahawk to parry the first downward stroke of the sword, igniting a spark as metal met metal and nimbly sidestepped the second. From the cabin roof, Squando shouted advice, "Fight like an Abenaki, like I taught." Barnabas dropped and entangled the large man like a scissors at his knees, tripping him over his own two legs. They tumbled together on the shore, but the large man far outweighed Barnabas. He had the young man pinned beneath him and was raising a meaty fist to pummel his face when his head snapped back with a crack, and his eyes rolled upward in his head. His heavy body slid off Barnabas, who rose shakily to his feet.

The Spanish girl stood on the shore with a long pole in her hands. Behind her, the flatboat began to drift. Her brother had finally brought the axe against the second mooring line. Barnabas seized the heavy pole from the girl, who appeared ready to swing it even harder against the head of the large man. He threw it instead to Squando on the deck. The current was already tugging the flatboat faster from the shore.

"Can you swim?" he turned to ask the girl but quickly turned away. She had shimmied out of her red skirt and draped it over her neck and shoulders. Then she plunged into the river without a word. She was struggling in deeper water when Barnabas, stroking hard, reached her side.

"Let me take your skirt. It drags you down." He reached out to take it from her, but she snapped, "I don't need your help." Yet she leaned against him in the water for a moment as she shaped the red skirt into a ball. She side-stroked with renewed strength, close enough to fling the ball of red cloth into her brother's outstretched hands. The youth promptly turned away from his sister, flailing in the water, to deposit the skirt into the cabin with their stowed canvas travel bags.

In disgust, Squando seized the pole and extended it into the girl's grasping hands, pulling her close enough to haul her, spluttering, onto the deck. Ramon arrogantly pushed him aside and escorted his bedraggled sister into the cabin, her man's sodden slouch hat still pinned to her head. Barnabas hauled himself onto the deck without any help. He and Squando exchanged a wordless look that said very clearly, "Women!"

With the young people engaged with the attack from the shore, the captain dropped through a trapdoor in the cabin roof and retrieved a blunderbuss, a short, powerful weapon common to all navies of the world. He climbed back onto the roof and pointed the gun at the port side rowboat, discharging its scatter shot into the terror-struck faces of the pirates below. The remaining crew of the other boat hastily brought it around and pulled furiously away.

At the captain's order, the rudder man brought the flatboat about to face down river, bow into the current. On the shore, they saw the wounded lantern bearer helping the large man stagger to his feet. Glaring after them, he shook his fist in impotent rage, shouting threats at the Spanish girl, who emerged from the cabin in her wet red skirt.

"No matter how far you go, Della, I'll track you down! I swear to God, no slip of a girl can rob Joe Fontaine!" She laughed in his face across the widening water. As the figures dwindled on the shore, the girl stepped back into the cabin, sat down on a bale and wept.

TWO

---·---

A HORSE RETURNS

They overshot their intended landing, and it took several hours of scanning the shore to find a suitable spot to beach. The Captain was eager to be rid of his troublesome passengers and anxious to regain a crew. The horses disembarked without fuss. The Spaniards retrieved their belongings and stepped off onto the shore. As the rudder man put the flatboat into the downstream current, the captain promptly turned his back on the young people left behind.

Squando mounted his plain brown horse and said to Barnabas in a significant tone, "Here is a good place to begin our journey west."

Although Barnabas recognized that Squando was not in favor of any further connection with the young Spaniards, he could not bring himself to abandon them on the inhospitable shore. He offered them Patrick and Henry to ride upriver into St. Louis. Squando scowled, but the young

Spaniard, with a sweeping bow, introduced himself and his sister.

"I have the honor to introduce my sister, Señorita Isabella Blanca Flores. I am Ramon Ignacio Flores. We are the daughter and son of the late merchant of New Orleans, Don Marco Alvarez Flores, and his also deceased wife, Dona Liliana Blanca Flores." The words flowed smoothly off his tongue.

Señor Ramon Flores then politely inquired as to the identities of these fellow travelers to whom he and his sister owed a great debt of gratitude. Squando and Barnabas exchanged a look, but Barnabas rose to the challenge.

"Señor Flores, I am honored to introduce my esteemed colleague, the widely known Prophet, Squando of the Turtle Clan of the Northern branch of the Abenaki, Vermont Territory. I, sir, am Barnabas Locke, courier, scout, and war veteran, son of the late Frederick Locke, merchant and landholder of the Vermont Territory." Barnabas was rather pleased with himself and doffed his hat and bowed to the señorita. The señorita responded with a cool nod.

Barnabas offered the young lady a leg up onto Henry, the smaller of the two pack horses. She frowned, looked inquiringly at Little Bay, but found herself heaved aboard. She settled herself among the sacks as though on a side saddle, arranging her red skirt around her. Barnabas noted that the folds of the rumpled cloth hung unevenly.

Ramon swung with a laugh onto Patrick's laden back, and the four riders turned north in the direction of St. Louis, where Barnabas and Squando intended a quick departure from their new acquaintances.

Woodland gave way to newly cultivated land. They struck a cart road through the countryside scattered with farm dwellings and barns. Surprisingly, they passed several large earthen mounds surrounded by furrowed fields. Squando and Barnabas recognized them as the remnants of a people who flourished here in a time before the incursions of Europeans. Not very long ago, the two friends had fought for their lives in the shadow of just such a mound in the Ohio Country.

By mid-day, they arrived on the streets of St. Louis, laid out by French settlers in a neat grid on a wide curve of the Mississippi River. Just to the north, the Missouri met the Mississippi. The señorita looked about with a particular interest. When they rode into the public center of the village, she spied the birch log church with a small bell tower topped with a cross. The señorita demanded an hour to pray and possibly, if the famous Father Bernard was in, to make confession. Pulling a small clinking pouch from her sash, she sent Ramon on a mission to locate two horses and the necessary tack.

Very prettily, she asked Barnabas, "Please accompany my brother as I believe you and Señor

Squando will better choose horses suitable for hard riding. My brother is too easily smitten by the fast, shiny ones," and she laughed charmingly. In light of Barnabas's quick agreement, she chose to ignore Squando's half-suppressed sigh and Ramon's visible irritation.

"Yes, Squando, I think we are good judges of horseflesh with, yes, one exception. Come, Ramon, let's go look at what horses St. Louis offers."

The public square, lined with businesses stretching down to the river, was busy with afternoon commerce. It must have been a market day as vendors hawked wares on all sides. Among them were farmers with livestock for sale—but only a few spavined horses among the pigs and chickens.

While Ramon bought hotcakes from a farmer's wife, Squando said quietly, "Barny, does it strike you strange that the young lady spends money for horses when they should be traveling down river?"

The same thought had occurred to Barnabas, but he was unwilling to question the señorita's intentions. Wasn't she in church at this very moment? Still, it was strange that she hadn't headed straight to the docks to book passage to New Orleans.

No horse met Squando's or Barnabas's standards for a lady. A helpful farmer directed them to a stable owned by his cousin. The liveryman shook his head at first, not eager to sell off good riding stock. But he had one horse he suspected he had misjudged. He did not misjudge the dandified young Spaniard.

"I do have a well-bred horse with very nice gaits that might please the young gentleman," he said, looking directly at Ramon. He disappeared into the stables and emerged soon after with a strapping, bright chestnut with four white stockings on a lead.

Squando choked back a howl. Barnabas looked thunderstruck. The chestnut preened and danced and arched his shiny neck, and Ramon fell in love. "This, this is the horse for me," he said. "We share the same spirit."

The young Spaniard would not listen to reason. He barely listened at all. He was too busy stroking the blazed face and cooing into the flicking ears. "I am a Spaniard. I know a fine horse when I see one."

This quirk of fate dumbfounded the two friends. They did not like or trust this horse. They already knew his vices. Barnabas had named him "Macaroni" as a slighting reference to his flashiness, and Squando had called him with contempt "that British horse." Now, they were suddenly saddled with him again, like an ill omen they could not shake.

Ramon would not be dissuaded and handed over an unseemly number of silver coins from the little pouch. Barnabas rescued some dignity from the transaction by negotiating a lesser price for an amiable, stocky and sound black horse about 15 hands tall at the withers. His common head was redeemed by a pretty white star. The liveryman promised, as horse dealers do, that he would make a sensible mount for a young lady. He was glad enough to be rid of the horse from Cahokia to haggle much. He sold them serviceable, well-oiled tack but had no sidesaddle. Ramon airily informed them that Señorita Isabella much preferred to ride astride when she could do so without compromising her reputation.

The three young men walked their string of horses back to the church yard, arriving just as Isabella opened the gate. She was fingering a small silver cross about her neck. She tucked the cross under her neck scarf and nodded in approval at the black horse, but when Macaroni danced elegantly in her direction, she, like her feckless brother, was smitten. "Yes," Barnabas thought to himself with regret, "the señorita is a practical young woman who loves pretty things too much."

The brother and sister squabbled over who should ride the bright chestnut. They made a spectacle of themselves outside the church gate. Isabella claimed for herself the privileges of being the elder, the one whose money had paid for the horse, and that she would show to very good advantage upon that horse. Ramon did not disagree with any of her arguments, but he made his case valiantly. Even the liveryman had recognized that he and the chestnut were a perfect match. Squando, who seldom spoke and never interfered in the disputes of other people, quietly made a suggestion. "Let the horse choose."

He took the reins and walked thirty paces away with the horse side-stepping fractiously at his side. Horse and man had disliked each other from their first meeting. Squando dropped the reins over the long mane. "Call out to your horse."

Isabella sang a stream of Spanish endearments. Ramon commanded him in the tone of authority. The horse flicked his ears dismissively at both of them. Ramon remembered what Barnabas had called the horse and spoke the name loudly.

"Macaroni. Come to me, my beauty." The youth could not guess that the horse had never responded to that name and resented it.

Isabella called out another name, one that came to her as if inspired and wafted its mellifluous notes across the thirty paces, "El Caballo Valiente." The horse lifted his showy head and nodded briskly three times, then trotted into her outstretched hands. "I called him 'the valiant horse,' and he came," she said proudly.

Squando muttered sourly, "That horse will never earn that name. She will find out what he really is." Ramon turned on his heels, defeated, and took the reins of the sturdy black horse. "Come, Segundo, we both come second."

The party stocked up in the marketplace on provisions, oats for the horses, necessary supplies and extra blankets. Somehow, without it being actually said aloud, the party seemed to have naturally expanded to four members. Squando waited with growing impatience for Barnabas to make farewells to the two young Spaniards. Instead, by dusk, they were still together, camped in a grove of cottonwoods miles beyond the village. Privately, Isabella approached Barnabas, laying a fine-fingered hand on his sleeve.

"With all my heart, I thank you, Señor Barnabas, for assisting us to St. Louis and for all your help, and that of Señor Squando, in acquiring horses and supplies. But I must ask a favor of you. Will you provide us with one more day of escort westward? Until there is distance between us and that rogue, Joe Fontaine, neither my brother nor I are safe." He did not doubt her.

Barnabas knew he was violating his pact with Squando by taking it upon himself to grant the señorita her request. Yet he did. It seemed to him impossible to abandon these unprotected young people to the hazard of pursuit by that large man he had wrestled with at the river, and the young lady had laid out flat with a pole to the back of his head. He admired her.

"What is your destination? Why not board a boat and hie yourselves south to New Orleans?

What sanctuary do you hope to find in this vast wilderness? This is no place for a lady like you. My friend and I are born for this country, but you are gently bred."

The señorita dropped her dark eyes in thought for a long moment. Then she raised them to look resolutely into his. "I swear to answer your questions tomorrow when we are a day's ride from this place."

THREE

ISABELLA'S STORY

Like a good soldier, Barnabas gingerly scraped the three-day stubble off his face with his folding razor. More water boiled for osage tea. Ramon was still tightly wrapped in his blanket. The señorita sat cross-legged on her bedroll, running a tortoiseshell comb through her luxuriant black hair. Barnabas watched as she twisted the thick coil into one long braid. She looked across the fire and smiled. "Good morning, Señor Barnabas." She tapped the corner of her jaw, and he hastily wiped his own jaw clean.

"What a fine scalp that would make hanging on the lodgepole of a Comanche warrior," Squando said in Abenaki. Returning into camp with the hobbled horses, he had caught the playful exchange between his friend and the exasperating señorita. Barnabas was startled by the matter-of-factness of his tone.

He hastened to reassure Squando, also in Abenaki. "I promised her only a day's escort.

We can give them that. We go our separate ways tomorrow." Squando looked askance at his friend.

The day's ride was surprisingly pleasant. The sun shone, the breeze was in their faces, blowing away gnats, and the high grass swayed over gentle rolling hills. El Caballo Valiente, previously Macaroni, obliged his new mistress. Barnabas rode in the rear with Patrick's lead line tied to his saddle and Henry trotting behind. At Ramon's urging, Squando demonstrated Indian hand talk, teaching the youth some of the basic signs. But they all paid attention.

"Friend," he said. "Hold your right hand so," and he demonstrated the right hand at the level of his neck, palm out, index and middle fingers touching and extending. "Then lift the right hand until the fingertips reach the level of your face." His motions were fluid and practiced. Ramon copied them exactly.

"Are you a friend?" Squando asked him. Before the youth could answer, they were distracted by the sudden rising of hundreds of geese, honking and circling above the crest of the grassy knolls ahead. "Feathers," Squando shouted and put his heels into the sides of his plain brown horse. Geese meant marshland, and marshland might mean river cane. Squando required river cane and feathers to fashion new arrows. Much of his supply, skillfully crafted over the winter months, had been lost repelling pirates at the river.

As Squando galloped ahead, the rest of the party loped after him, arriving at the crest of the highest knoll where Squando had brought his horse to a dead halt. They, too, were stunned by the spectacle of hundreds, if not thousands, of buffalo, fording a tributary in the swale below them. The feeding geese had risen in protest. The cows, their winter coats in tattered clumps, were solicitous of their bleating red calves, urging them into the water and nudging them up the hoof-churned bank on the other side. Young bulls noisily tested their strength against each other in mock battle, and the old bulls paced alertly, snuffing the air on the alert for predators. The riders above watched in silent fascination as the columns of buffalo crossed the wide stream in a seemingly endless procession.

"I'll catch up with you," Squando said to Barnabas, who turned the party reluctantly westward again.

Before dusk, Squando rejoined the riders with two fat geese for dinner and a bundle of strong river cane for his arrow shafts. He was in a very good mood, although, on principle, he did not show it.

When they camped for the night under willows where the stream narrowed, all hands joined in plucking the geese. Squando collected the primary feathers, separating the left wing from the right wing, for his fletching. Ramon cheerfully took charge of turning the spit over a fire fueled with dried dung, which he had not so cheerfully gathered. When he pronounced dinner ready, they ate the roasted meat greedily with their hands, sopping up the grease with hardtack biscuits.

After their meal, Squando began to shape his fletching with a dangerously sharp obsidian knife, a prized tool he carried with him. Ramon pestered him for more hand-talk signs. Barnabas sent Isabella a significant look, indicating he was ready to hear her story. She rose to her feet, shook out her red skirt, and cleared her throat to signal she was about to speak. She stood behind the fire so that the reflection of the flames would light her face in the growing dark.

"I promised to tell the story of how my brother Ramon and I came to be in this wild place with two strangers who are becoming friends." Ramon's face betrayed immediate alarm. She smiled at him reassuringly and continued.

"Our late Father, Don Flores, was born into a distinguished merchant family in Mexico City. His family sent him to Spain for his education. Then, as a promising young merchant, to New Orleans to establish another branch of their mercantile house, La Casa de Flores. There, fortunately for us, he married our beloved Mother. After our Mother's untimely death, I was sent away to be convent-educated, and Ramon was tutored at our family home in Mexico City. Our Father's business was founded on trade with overseas markets in Seville, Barcelona, and Marseilles. These are insatiable markets for fur, hides, and showy feathers. To meet that demand, he made connections with men who were not always honorable. In short, he employed the services of Joe Fontaine, whom you met on the banks of the Mississippi." She paused to take a breath and then plunged into the rest of her story.

"Alas, the uncertainties and disruptions in trade occasioned by the War between the colonies and Great Britain created serious financial difficulties for my Father. He was already over-extended in his commitments. War is not good for business. Then, when France, followed by Spain, came into the War on the side of the Americans, both to vex their great enemy England and to secure their vast land holdings in this New World, his business verged on collapse. Foreseeing the growth of commerce as people pour across the Mississippi River, he liquidated his properties in New Orleans and invested in portable wealth to start anew elsewhere, possibly in St. Louis."

Here, she pulled from the seam of her waistband a jewel the size of a bird's egg, sparkling red in the firelight. She handed the ruby to Barnabas, who, in turn, tossed the bauble to Squando. The Abenaki snatched it from the air, examined it against the flames, grunted softly, and then tossed it to Ramon.

The señorita retrieved the ruby from her brother's hands and tucked it back into her waistband. She continued her story. "He had many creditors, my poor Father, none more pressing than Joe Fontaine, whose piracy along the Ohio River had helped to keep my Father's business solvent. I would like to tell you that my Father was innocent of any such knowledge, but his actions reveal that he was not. Early last year, he traveled secretly overland, taking every precaution, to the very village we have recently left, St. Louis. On Spanish territory with Spanish soldiers to protect its inhabitants, he sought out his old friend, Father Bernard, and entrusted into his godly hands a small fortune in gems, among them this ruby. He envisioned new opportunities in this pathway to the west. Naturally, he did not confide his ambitions to Joe Fontaine, but that man has spies. When my Father crossed the river to Cahokia to repay his debt to him with coins, and this very ruby, Joe Fontaine guessed there was more to be had. It grieves me to my heart to tell you what happened next. When Joe Fontaine pressed my Father for more of his wealth, my brave Father resisted. A man of vicious impulse, Joe Fontaine murdered our Father with that same sword he used against you at the river." Overcome, Isabella struggled to regain her composure. When she was sure of her voice, she continued.

"My brother and I received the tragic news of our Father's death from Father Bernard, along

31

with a letter our Father had providentially left in his keeping. From that letter, we verified the rumors that Joe Fontaine was the likely agent of his death. We swore a solemn oath to seek out that villain, to confirm he was the murderer, and to avenge our Father with his death. When we arrived in Cahokia, we assumed aliases Diego and Della Ramirez to gain entry into Joe Fontaine's gang of cutthroats and criminals. To win his confidence, we violated our principles. I flaunted myself at him while keeping him at arm's length. I enticed gullible men to his card tables, encouraged them to drink, and enabled Ramon to fleece them at cards. He is very quick with his hands."

Squando had laid down his knife. Barnabas sat entranced. Even Ramon, who knew the story, listened intently as his sister exposed their secrets to strangers.

The señorita resumed. "When I made sure of the opportunity, I rifled through his quarters and found my Father's initialed pistol. I needed no other evidence of Joe Fontaine's guilt. I took the gun. The pistol was primed, and I waited for Joe Fontaine to return. I planned to confront him, wrest his confession from him, and then kill him with my Father's pistol. While I waited upstairs, I picked his locked strongbox with my Mother's emerald hatpin, which I always wear on my head. The box was under the villain's bed, hidden by buffalo robes. Inside, I found my Father's purse, the one my dear Mother embroidered his initials upon, with the silver and gold coins and this ruby with which my Father had paid Joe Fontaine. I took that, too, and this pretty silver bracelet as it was just lying there." Here, she raised her arm to admire the flash of the bracelet in the firelight.

She continued. "Downstairs, Ramon deliberately lost money at the gaming table. He staged an angry outburst as a signal that Joe Fontaine had entered the room below. But things went badly. As I told you, Joe Fontaine is a man with an ugly temper. He seized my brother and began to beat him. I tucked the pistol and the purse into hidden pockets sewn into my skirt. I hurried down the stairs into the gaming room. Joe Fontaine might have killed Ramon had I not interceded. I flung myself between them and slapped Joe Fontaine hard across his face and then again. He recoiled in disbelief. Then the bully laughed at me. I seized my brother's arm and hurried him out of that place into the light of day."

She sat down trembling. "Yesterday, Father Bernard gave me good advice, as well as absolution for my sins. He has given me a letter of introduction to a Franciscan friar he trusts in Santa Fe, where he advises we seek refuge. He bids us go at once and to cover our tracks. If God looks after us, Joe Fontaine will be judged by his Maker. While he lives, he remains a danger to us and very likely to the good Father. His cassock would be no defense against that evil man. He or his agents have already violated our Father's grave. Father Bernard promises to send a message to our uncle in Mexico City that we are on the way to him on the overland trail through Santa Fe. Our uncle will provide an armed escort from there so that we may later safely return to St. Louis to retrieve our inheritance hidden by Father Bernard. If you help us on our journey there, this ruby is yours."

Barnabas rose and began to kick out the fire, which had dwindled to embers. He had questions that he did not choose to ask the señorita. Her business was hers. "Squando and I must think on your proposal. I ain't a man who hankers after riches. Squando wants only to escape the white man's world and the visions that trouble his mind. Tomorrow, we give our answer."

FOUR

YOUNG RAVEN

Squando and Barnabas stood alone, talking in the prairie grass. Isabella was dividing the remains of the geese for a cold breakfast. The young men naturally assumed meals were her duty. Although not amused, she undertook the role of camp cook as her contribution. Ramon was currying the hobbled horses, lingering longingly over Valiente's bright coat. The two friends walked back into camp with unreadable faces.

Squando raised his hand, signaling that he was about to speak on a serious matter. He looked at Ramon. "I asked you yesterday, 'are you my friend?' Now I ask for your reply."

"I think you would be a good friend and a good teacher. I would be honored to claim your friendship," Ramon replied with dignity.

"Then it is so. I would not leave a friend unprotected in the wilderness." He turned to Isabella. "I need no pretty stone. Friends pay each other with good actions." It was a gentle rebuke, but she was not offended.

In the ensuing days, the party of four young people traveled across endless miles of open tall-grass. The sun shone, the wind was warm, and migrating birds flew north in uncountable numbers. Bees harvested the pollen of spring flowers blooming across the prairie. Larks sang. Pronghorn antelope, spying them from miles away, kept a safe distance. During the day, either Squando or Barnabas backtracked for several miles to hunt and scout for pursuers. Squando began to point out signs of Indians who had traveled this way before them, following the buffalo, he opined. He could number the riders and the walkers and even discern the faint track of travois through the grass, useful for packing buffalo meat and hides. His lessons in hand talk intensified. Ramon was his best pupil. Against his will, Squando warmed to the young Spaniard.

"We have seen no people of the plains, only their sign. But they have seen us. We must know how to show our peaceful intentions. By nearly the same sign, you give your name or ask another's name, and he demonstrated by the fluid motion of his right hand to his students.

Squando's prediction materialized as an aged man on foot, wrapped in a striped blanket. He appeared like a spirit being out of the dusk, with none of the horses signaling his arrival at their campfire. Likely, he had been drawn by the scent of the roasting antelope Barnabas had shot that morning.

The Indian was shriveled and small, wrinkled and white-haired, but his back was erect and his smile wide and peaceable. His black eyes snapped with good humor. Squando rose from his arrow making to hand-sign a welcome. The old man named his tribe by first brushing his left hand over the back of his outstretched right hand, the sign for "Indian." Then he closed his right hand into a fist and tapped it two times against the left side of his chest, the sign for "mother," indicating that he was proudly Arapaho, "the mother of all the tribes." Apparently, the Arapaho had a very high opinion of their rank amongst their neighbors.

Isabella heaped her empty plate with choice bits of meat and offered it to their guest. She indicated that he should take her seat by the fire. To give her name, she tightly closed her right hand and held it in front of her face, with her thumb touching the other fingers and knuckles pointing towards the old man. Then she pointed her index finger inward at the same time moving her right hand slightly towards herself. She said clearly in Spanish, "I am Belle." Then she repeated the sign to ask the old man his name by pointing her index finger and moving her right fist slightly towards him.

The old man chuckled in approval. He replied, "Oh-has-tee," as he made the hand talk signs for "Young Raven." "Now, Old Raven," and he made the sign of an old person leaning on a stick and bending forward. The three young men then offered their names, and in a mix of Spanish, English, French, and hand talk, they conversed together after the Raven had eaten his fill.

Squando asked him why he traveled alone on foot. The Arapaho admitted that, while he slept, his two horses had been stolen, possibly by Pawnees, but spoke with admiration for the thieves' prowess. He had been on foot for two days when he crossed their trail and considered stealing two of their horses, as he had often done as a young warrior counting coup. He indicated with a gnarled thumb the hobbled Valiente and shook his head. "Not that one."

The old fellow signed that he would sleep now. He rolled himself in his blanket and was soon gently snoring. The young people were astonished by his sudden presence at their campfire, horseless in this vastness yet seemingly unperturbed. Would he prove a burden or a benefit? Squando determined to mine him for information as soon as he politely could.

In the morning, Squando shifted some of Patrick's load to Henry, clearing room on Patrick's back for the Raven. When he scrambled up, the old man looked no more than another large sack. Squando on his plain brown horse rode alongside, using hand talk and common words in Spanish and French. The Spanish had brought the gift of horses in the time of the distant grandfathers, the Raven said. The French brought guns. Trade went better when each party understood the other. Always of interest, the topic of horses arose. The Raven asked the name of the horse he was riding. Informed the horse was called "Patrick," the old man looked dissatisfied.

"'Pat Rick,'" he repeated slowly. "It has no meaning. What does it tell about this horse?"

Squando's forehead furrowed. "He is a pack horse. My friend named him and the other after a great hero of their war, Patrick Henry, though neither horse has proved himself brave." He shrugged. "Barny believes horses require a name. He reminds me that my horse," and he patted the neck of the plain brown horse beneath him, "has no name. I tell him I will name my horse when he earns that name."

The old Arapaho ruminated for some while in silence. "It is true," he said eventually, "that some horses are more worthy of a good name, even if they are not good but are very bad." The Raven pointed first to Barnabas and then to Isabella, riding companionably ahead. "Man and wife?"

Squando said, "They think they are friends. I see something more."

"I had wives. Most were good wives. All are dead. My lodge is empty." The old man looked thoughtful.

They were now a party of five. They traveled always with the wind in their faces and the grasses like waves surging towards them. They rode west towards mountains the old Arapaho described as a great jagged wall rising above the plains, wearing snow through every season. In the lengthening evenings, the Raven regaled his young audience with tales of his youth and manhood spent distinguishing himself in the military society to which he had belonged since boyhood. He told how he had graduated with his cohort of boys herding horses, to youths learning the fine art of stealing them, to warriors counting coup and hunting buffalo on their backs. "I gained much honor," he said. "Now I am old and retired."

He was returning from a vision quest he told them. Lately, he had been troubled by strange, unsettling dreams. He set out on a vision quest to the east, suspecting that white men were the source of those dreams. He traveled with his two remaining horses—he had honorably given away the rest—as far as the Great River. The river was no longer a boundary or a barrier. White people were moving westward and building settlements. He foresaw another kind of trespass.

He chuckled, saying, "Now I have no horses, but I have new friends." Squando, deeply moved, engaged the old man privately in conversations about dreams, how to decipher them, and how to use them for good.

One day, in the heat of early summer, Barnabas turned Little Bay back on their tracks. As he had done nearly every day, he rode to hunt game and to look for any sign of pursuit. He rode through a series of ravines and topping one he saw unshod horse tracks in the dust. Six distinct sets of tracks traveled from the southeast in a northwesterly direction. Whoever made those tracks would soon come upon their own set of fresh tracks headed due west. He went cautiously forward, stretched out on Little Bay to lower his silhouette, and riding parallel below the ridge lines. Before he topped a ridge, he dismounted, ground-tied Little Bay by dropping his reins, and cautiously climbed upwards, his rifle at the ready, to peer over the crest into the distance.

His heart paused a long moment when he saw six dismounted men, young warriors of what tribe he could not say, closely examining what he guessed to be the fresh tracks of his party. He took a long look, noting the details of the small band, and then skittered down the slope, mounted Little Bay, and galloped his gallant little horse hell-bent for leather back to his friends.

When he reached them, he flew past, shouting "Hostiles!" and gesturing them to gallop onward behind him. Even Henry, heavily laden and bringing up the rear, kept pace. Barnabas looked for some shelter—a rock outcropping, a grove of cottonwood, a dry wash—but the tallgrass waved on relentlessly. After several miles at a hard gallop, he signaled for a breather. He counted the number of their weapons. His Jaeger rifle and pistol, both already primed and loaded, Squando's pistol and his deadly accurate bow, and Isabella's father's pistol. Ramon and the Raven carried only their knives. Each of the six Indians now doubtless in pursuit carried bows and lances. Two also carried muskets.

The old Arapaho signed for a description of the six warriors. Through Squando, Barnabas described the boldly painted bodies of both men and horses, the eagle feathers braided in their manes, and the distinctive hair of the warriors—cut horizontally from the lower outside edge of the eyes to the back of their ears.

The Raven nodded in recognition. "Kiowa," he said, "very bad." And he made the sign for the Kiowa—holding two straight fingers near the lower outside edge of his right eye and moving those two fingers past his ear.

Squando was the first to spy horses fast approaching across the prairie. They kicked their mounts towards the slope of a low hill for the advantage of firing from higher ground with the sun behind them. That was all they could do to prepare for the onslaught. As they neared the top of the rise, however, they were brought to an abrupt halt. Six warriors on horseback dominated the skyline just above them. Their bodies were tattooed with red circles on their upper chest. They raised their bows to the sky in unison, launching a volley of arrows down upon the Kiowas. The Kiowas answered in kind.

The Raven shouted triumphantly, "Warriors of my tribe," and he gave throat to a reedy war cry. The party swung about to face the Kiowas as the Arapahos galloped downhill past them, screaming into battle against sworn enemies. Squando drew his bow and let loose two arrows in swift succession, both of them striking one of the Kiowa outriders, trying to escape the hail of arrows. Shouting his Abenaki war cry, he kicked his plain brown horse down the slope, plunging without hesitation into the fight. As he rode by the dead Kiowa, he leaned low to count coup by yanking out one of his arrows piercing the body. He left the other as a sign that an Abenaki warrior had claimed this Kiowa's life, a man who had ridden boldly into the Arapaho ambush.

Barnabas, too, rode into the thick of the melee of thrusting lances, flying arrows, and gun shots.

His pistol fire struck one Kiowa, who swung his horse away, leaning low over its neck. Barnabas brought up his rife, aimed at the zigzagging wounded warrior, and shot him dead at a hundred paces. The rifle spent, he used its butt to club down a dismounted warrior who leaped against Little Bay to wrest him from the saddle. He held on while a grinning Arapaho ran his lance through the man's back. Suddenly, it seemed the field of battle lay silent under the sun. Arapaho warriors walked among the dead Kiowas, taking scalps and trophies. One young warrior was sent to round up fleeing horses.

Through the rush of blood in his head, Barnabas heard Isabella calling frantically to him. He rode swiftly back up the rise to her side. As he dismounted, she flung herself upon him, distraught, crying out, "Ramon is dying! He is bleeding to death." Barnabas shook her off and dropped to his knees beside the youth, an arrow protruding through his left thigh, his leg awash in the swift flow of arterial blood. His breath came in short gasps. Tears of pain streaked his blanched face. Barnabas signed to the Raven to hold Ramon still. He yanked the scarf from Isabella's neck and wrapped it above the wound at a pressure point. Ignoring Ramon's cries, he quickly broke the arrow and used the long end as a crank to tighten the pressure of the tourniquet. From his neck, he pulled his neckerchief, twirling it into two knots at either end. The Raven skillfully pulled the short end of the arrow from the boy's thigh while Barnabas pushed the knotted ends of his neckerchief into the entry and exit wounds. He wrapped the length of cloth remaining into a tight bandage about the leg. The flow of red blood abated.

Barnabas had learned on the battlefield that a tourniquet must be loosened every five minutes to allow blood to flow naturally to the extremities. He showed Isabella how to do this. She was thankful to be of service to her brother, who looked up at her reassuring smile with shocked, scared eyes.

Squando, leading a Kiowa-painted horse, joined Barnabas and the old Arapaho. The Raven was held in high respect by these warriors and was obeyed. Already, he had ordered that a travois be fashioned to transport Ramon to his home village, where he had been subtly directing his young friends ever since he appeared at their campfire.

Time seemed to stop until the deputized Arapahos returned with suitable young saplings. Under the old man's supervision, a serviceable travois was speedily constructed and affixed to Ramon's saddle. Segundo stamped his feet and kicked out only once and then settled into his new burden. Isabella had collected their blankets to make a cushion into which Barnabas and Squando gently lifted Ramon, gritting his teeth in growing pain.

The young warrior had returned with three of the Kiowa horses. The party of Arapaho was well-pleased with their exploits this summer day. They had cleverly executed an ambush, had counted coup and defeated worthy adversaries. They would arrive at their village with horses, scalps, an esteemed returning veteran and his adopted friends. When they next rode out on a mission, they would paint their horses in bright colors with the symbols of these successes.

The combined parties, with Barnabas and Isabella walking on either side of the travois, set out towards the Raven's home village. Behind them, vultures circled.

FIVE

GOOD MEDICINE

The Raven's home village had stood within its palisade in a wooded bottomland since before his birth. Springs bubbled under the cottonwoods. The vast peak of Sun Mountain, called Tava Kaa-vi by the Utes, gleamed white in the distance. The Raven occupied the earth lodge of his maternal grandmother, a home for three generations, now empty but for this one old man, whose wives and sons had died before him. His daughters had married outside the village. Aged out of his military society, the lone survivor of his cohort, the Raven had been feeling melancholy and restless. He had left on a quest to seek the aid of the spirit beings and had returned with young people in need of him.

The Raven had sent word ahead of an arrow wound, and the medicine man was prepared with the necessary ointments, ingredients, and secretly-held remedies in his medicine bundle. A brusk man of middle age, his first words were a disclaimer. "Good medicine for Arapahos, maybe not so good for a yellow hide." He looked askance at Isabella, hovering over Ramon with damp cloths, and ordered her out of the lodge. "Later," he said to her, and the Raven gently hustled her through the short entry passage and the hide flap.

The medicine man set to work removing the soiled bandaging and cleaning away the blood encrusted at the entry and exit wounds. After two days of hard jouncing in a travois, the thigh was badly swollen, and Ramon was sweating profusely from a climbing fever. He was drifting in and out of consciousness and thrashing from the pain. The medicine man rose from his initial examination with some encouraging words. "No bad smell, no bad color." He instructed Squando to assist in removing all of Ramon's clothing to be burned. Any residue of bad spirits could cling to the garments, which had to be burnt away from the village. The medicine man looked closely at the silver cross around Ramon's neck. He was familiar with the Spanish religion and chose not to meddle with a potentially powerful spiritual being.

He proceeded to heat a pair of long porcupine quills over the fire. When they were hot to the touch, he instructed Squando to hold Ramon still. As Barnabas held a lamp—tallow in a turtle shell—close overhead, the medicine man simultaneously lanced a hot quill into each of the pus sacs formed at the two sites, bursting them. He pressed hard to extract pus and blood. Ramon screamed, then fell limp into his blankets. Isabella cried out from the other side of the passage, but the Raven refused her admittance.

Deliberately, the medicine man uncovered a clay pot and scooped out a poultice concocted of yarrow leaves, willow bark, and bitterroot, all with known properties for clotting blood and reducing fever and swelling. He unrolled a length of soft fawn skin to wrap the leg securely. "Call in the woman," he instructed Squando.

Isabella accepted from his hands a gourd with a wooden stopper and a horn cup. Through Squando, whom he had identified at once as the most qualified of these strangers, he instructed Isabella to mix a thumb full, indicating with his thumb the contents from the stoppered gourd with water in the horn cup. "Repeat until the gourd is empty."

As Isabella knelt at Ramon's side, the medicine man beckoned the others into the daylight. "The spirit beings may claim this young man. Fever may take him. I will return in the morning. If his fever continues high, it would be wise to have Blue Smoke conduct a healing ceremony. Do you have tobacco? He will need tobacco. And a fee." The medicine man turned towards his lodge, taking Squando's Kiowa horse with him in payment.

By morning, the fever had not broken. Ramon burned, then shook with chills. He had begun to rave, in strange detail, about treasure. He saw nuggets of gold lying in creek beds, seams of silver, and stones of bright blue. Isabella was sleepless and distraught. The medicine man returned as promised, renewed the poultice, and instructed Isabella to fill the horn cup more frequently, although it was difficult to get any of its contents down Ramon's throat. "Send for Blue Smoke," he urged. A youth, eager to earn status, volunteered to fetch him.

When not at Ramon's side, Isabella paced, fingering the delicate silver cross at her throat as she fervently said her prayers. While it was still light, the youth returned with Blue Smoke, an individual conscious of his considerable standing in his widespread community. He was dressed in lavishly beaded soft leather, eagle feathers adorned his oiled long hair, and a streak of purple swept over his strong nose and cheeks. Broad silver armbands pocked with blue stones encircled his arms. He carried with him the sacred bundle of his calling. The spiritual healer appeared unwilling to step inside the lodge before receiving his fee.

Barnabas had searched through their trade goods and retrieved several twists of aromatic tobacco, which Blue Smoke accepted as his due. He waved away the small mirrors, the glass beads, and the calico cloth that Barnabas laid before him.

"Women's things," he said disdainfully. His quick eyes caught the gleam of silver around Isabella's exposed neck, and he pointed to the little silver cross on its silver chain. He challenged her. "Is your creator's medicine stronger than mine?"

Isabella was quick to read his meaning and pulled from her waistband the robin's egg-sized ruby, holding it aloft to catch the gleam of the late afternoon light. Blue Smoke's eyes sparkled as brightly as the ruby. He palmed the stone as his fee. Then, surprisingly to the young observers, he stripped down to loincloth and moccasins and only then entered the lodge to examine his new patient.

In the dim light inside, he immediately sprinkled sweetgrass liberally around the sickbed. Its sweet, piquant scent perfumed the air. "The sacred hair of Mother Earth," the Raven informed them in a reverential voice. Onto the fire, Blue Smoke tossed handfuls of sage. The Raven said wisely, "Sage draws bad spirits out of the body." At the doorway, Blue Smoke stationed the youth who had escorted him and charged him with tapping a small drum in a steady, rhythmic cadence. "The drum calls to the bad spirits," the Raven told them. Outside the door, Blue Smoke posted four women of the village, armed with stiff brooms and practiced in ritual healings.

Throughout the night, Blue Smoke chanted in a mesmerizing drone, never stopping even as he replenished the sweetgrass on the earth floor and the sage in the fire. He watched Ramon intently for any change in the labored rise and fall of his chest, in the whites of his eyes, and in the odor of his exhaling breath. As weary hours passed from night to dawn, the hypnotic chant, the drumming, and the heavy competing scents lulled the watchers into a stupor. This, too, Blue Smoke observed with interest. Only the Raven and the drumming boy remained alert.

As the first fingers of dawn penetrated the lodge through the open flap, Blue Smoke judged Ramon ready to expel his body's bad spirits. He lit the first of several of the tobacco twists, waving each twist seductively under the youth's nose and mouth, wafting the smoke in the direction of the open doorway. The Raven intoned softly, "Wakan Tanka, hear our prayer." As Blue Smoke lit the last of the tobacco twists, Ramon groaned deep in his chest, half-rose from his sweat-soaked blankets, and expelled a plume of foul matter into the laden air. As the climax of fever and smoke met and mingled above Ramon's body, Blue Smoke motioned to the young drummer to exit the lodge, drumming ever faster and harder. Blue Smoke enticed the plume from the bedside and through the short passage into the light of dawn. The women waiting outside the flap pounced on the plume of smoke and matter, breaking it apart and scattering it to the four winds. They whacked and slashed until there was nothing but sweet air beneath their brooms.

The young people groggily regained their senses just as Ramon fell into sleep. Only cloudy impressions of the exorcism remained. Except for the peaceful Ramon, they were routed from the lodge by the four women. Efficiently, they swept away the sweetgrass, sage, and lingering smoke—all of them tainted by the banished spirit. On a long stick, they flung Ramon's soiled blankets out of the lodge, wrapping him in a clean one. They spread fresh sweetgrass around Ramon's sleeping form, singing a ritual song of well-being. They left the lodge, giggling and smiling, content with Isabella's liberality of payment in mirrors, glass beads, and a bolt of calico cloth, the very "women's things" that Blue Smoke had disdained.

SIX

HUNTING BUFFALO

Blue Smoke, again dressed in his fine buckskins, and the Raven left the lodge together to consult with other village elders about the summer buffalo hunt. The Raven's return to the village was seen as a propitious sign, and Blue Smoke was prepared to ritually address Wakan Tanka, the Great Mystery, to bless the hunt. The Raven suggested that the American and the Abenaki warrior be invited to join the hunt in light of their valor in the fight against the Kiowa raiding party.

Barnabas and Squando welcomed the invitation to take part in the life of the community. As in the other Arapaho villages, the people here—some one hundred souls—made ready for the hunt. It was the largest communal enterprise of the year and the one on which much of their well-being through the winter depended. Travois were packed. Juniper wood was gathered for fires to roast and dry buffalo meat to make pemmican. Pegs were sharpened for the stretching of buffalo hides. Butchering knives were finely edged. Hunters restocked lances and arrows, each with its mark of ownership, for the great race across the prairie alongside their massive prey. Everyone was busy with some task to ensure the success of the hunt.

Ramon was on his feet, although leaning heavily on a crutch that Barnabas fashioned for him with the advice of the Raven. Isabella had moved into the lodge of the four widows, who took the two young Spaniards under their protection. They were busy making new sets of buckskins for their charges. Used to feminine company as she had been in her strict convent, here Isabella found a sisterhood more to her liking—one of joking and laughing and storytelling while adept fingers flew over their work.

Before the scattered bands assembled at the appointed rendezvous, both Barnabas and Squando were invited to join scouting forays with the six members of the Red Circle cohort of Arapaho. Those young warriors were readily identified by the distinctive tattoo etched on their upper chest. Young Raven bore those same circles on his chest; the red faded with the years. The two friends wondered if they were eligible for admission into the Red Circle fraternity. They determined to acquit themselves honorably during the buffalo hunt to earn that honor. Under the particular tutelage of

Two Rivers, the member most friendly to them, Squando and Barnabas became conversant with the Arapaho language and social etiquette and more practiced in hand talk.

Under auspicious skies, the four bands of Arapaho men and women gathered in a fever of anticipation, together with a number of visiting Cheyenne, close allies and trading partners specializing in buffalo hides. Blue Smoke shone in glory, a bright red stone sewn securely on the exterior of the amulet bag around his neck. A full day and night were devoted to dancing to an insistent drumbeat, singing and chanting, and smoking the pipe to send the sacred smoke of tobacco toward Wakan Tanka. Hunters immersed themselves in the smoke to disguise their human scent and to seek protection by the spirit beings. They painted white circles around the eyes and nostrils of their ponies to strengthen their senses.

Unlike his usually reserved self, Barnabas entered whole-heartedly into the communal fervor. He painted Little Bay with the symbols of power. Squando forged connections between his Abenaki ritual beliefs and those of the Arapaho.

When scouts reported the location of the gathering herd, the two friends rode with the Red Circle among the many other cohorts from all four bands. There was prestige to be earned, and every warrior turned hunter sought his share of honors.

No hunter wanted to be the careless spark causing a premature stampede. They rode their ponies by stealth along the growing perimeter of the herd, concentrating on moving the columns of buffalo into one mass of lumbering beasts. Those hunters chosen to direct the buffalo in the appointed direction were disguised as buffalo themselves, wearing hides and horns.

When bulls caught the unmistakeable scent of humans, sensed the excitement of the ponies, and were spooked by unnatural movements on the hillsides, their growing unease flowed through the herd like a struck tuning fork. Instantaneously, unease bloomed into panic, the herd surging into a stampede. The hunt was on.

Barnabas chose his buffalo for its unscarred hide, bringing Little Bay side by side, the horse matching strides with the behemoth that dwarfed him. The buffalo's small eye bored into Little Bay's. The game little horse was not intimidated. The beast veered suddenly into his path. Little Bay swung wide and then drew close again. Barnabas had the one shot with the powerful Jaeger. Using the rifle like a pistol extending from his arm, he brought the muzzle down to the heart of his prey and fired the precious shot. The buffalo stumbled and fell, dead before he hit the ground. Barnabas flung down his sharpened marker, bearing a tattered flounce of Isabella's red skirt. As Little Bay slowed, Barnabas reloaded the Jaeger, using the economical motions he had practiced for days. Within moments, he was back in the hunt, stalking another great-humped and bearded beast. He brought down two more before Little Bay signaled he was spent.

Buffalo fell in a cloud of dust and buffalo stink, the deafening rumble of hooves diminishing as the herd outran the hunters. The pursuers slowed their exhausted ponies. Across the plains for several long miles, heaps of giant brown bodies lay in the sun. The women swarmed onto the killing field, slaying the bleating calves, separated from their mothers, and wielding their butchering knives in a race against flies. Their work would continue into the night. As Barnabas rode Little Bay back to the first of his kills, he was hailed by a jubilant Isabella working alongside her four widows. Barnabas's fallen buffalo were theirs.

Squando rode into their circle, his plain brown horse lathered, breathing hard and limping. One shoulder was bloodied from a deep gash, a flap of skin hanging loose. "He didn't stop," Squando boasted, sliding off his nameless horse. "He was fearless."

One of the widows dug into a pouch and drew out a heavy bone needle already threaded with sinew. Quickly and skillfully, she stitched the flap of skin back into place, rinsed the wound clean with water, dried it gently with a length of fawn skin, and applied an ointment. Barnabas noticed it smelled very much like the ointment she applied to Ramon's healing wound. Squando held his horse's head close against his own, murmuring words of praise. When he raised his head, his eyes were suspiciously damp.

"My horse is Fearless. He has earned his name. I will paint a great red circle on his chest to show his strong heart."

SEVEN

TATTOOS

High summer waned into early fall. Women throughout the four bands had devoted their time to drying and seasoning pemmican from buffalo meat, to harvesting sinew and bone and horns for practical uses, and to the scraping, stretching, and sewing together of hides. It was work done companionably in the shade cast by cottonwood trees. Isabella cheerfully undertook her share of the labor at the lodge of the four widows. Cheyenne intermediaries purchased many of those hides, including the unmarked ones cleanly brought down by Barnabas and Squando. The payment in high-quality trade goods was shared equitably among the hunters and the women who prepared the hides.

With their share of the wealth, Barnabas and Squando sought to purchase their initiation into the Red Circle rung of the village military society. The Raven discussed the matter with other village elders, who commented favorably on the candidates' success in the summer buffalo hunt. Two Rivers had witnessed their bravery in battle with the Kiowas and sponsored their admission into the Red Circle.

Squando and Barnabas joined the six members of the Red Circle in a long soak in the sweat lodge. Blue Smoke officiated at the ceremony. The best of the village tattooists, a married woman named Quill Woman, practiced her painstaking art on the tender flesh of their upper chests. With cactus needles, she pricked the circular design into their skin, dipping the needles into a secret paste recipe—possibly a mixture of beebalm, sumac fruit, and sycamore bark— yielding a pleasing permanent red dye. Using a template of birch bark, she applied the distinctive design—a circle about the size of a small child's fist. From its perimeter, rays ran in varying lengths, each ray signifying a significant exploit. Two Rivers bore two tattoos with space enough for more rays to commemorate future victories.

Quill Woman was intrigued by the blank canvas of Squando's plucked pate, although he declined her invitation to tattoo it. Tiva, her marriageable daughter and talented apprentice, mischievously mocked Squando for his style in hair—plucked across the front and sides to the neck with a thick topknot pierced with feathers of his choosing. Her luxuriant mane was bound in two glossy braids that hung in loops decorated with small white shells. She was a dancing sort of sweet-faced girl. Squando and she traded gibes and jokes, not quite flirting but making each other laugh. Barnabas watched Squando's solemn face lighten and brighten in her company. But he foresaw no bridal dancing for pretty Tiva.

Already, Squando and Barnabas had earned rays for the battle with the Kiowas and their impressive buffalo count. They were granted another for the past battle on the Great River with the pirates, a story whose popularity never waned at the evening storytelling. The young men endured the ordeal stoically and were pleased with the results. Payments to Blue Smoke and Quill Woman and the steep initiation fee into the Red Circle quickly depleted their reserves.

Ramon would not be denied his tattoo. He wanted the concentric circles of the Arapaho design in the traditional blue color. Not on his shoulder or torso, but around both the entry and exit scars the Kiowa arrow had left permanently on his thigh. "It will be my badge of honor," he boasted. He found stoicism harder to achieve than his older friends but acquitted himself well. Isabella gave him a quilled belt to pay Quill Woman's fee.

Squando joined with Two Rivers and his fellow Red Circle cohort in hunting the eastern slopes of the terrifying range of mountains rising in the distance. He acquired a growing stockpile of quality elk and deer hides and soft beaver pelts. Around the evening campfires, he shared the disturbing prophecies that had driven him first from his own Green Mountains and then exiled him from the Ohio Country. He recounted visions of many chimneys where there had been none, of forests felled to make fields, and of whistling clouds of smoke coming up and down the Great River. White people were always on the move. He felt bound by honor to warn his new community of what dangers were coming with the white man.

One vision in particular held them spellbound, an image that Squando likened to a white serpent. He saw unending lines of great, rattling wooden wagons covered with white canvas crossing the grasslands. They brought families of yellow hides looking for new lands to divide amongst themselves to plow and plant and to deny the buffalo their passage.

"Our peoples will be displaced from their lands. I have seen it twice over across the Great River to the east. It has happened to my Abenaki people," he said. His listeners heeded the warning in this vision. Squando advised them to hold fast to their traditional alliances with their kind. Older, wiser heads nodded in approval. The younger men were not as convinced. They liked the power that guns brought them.

Barnabas was restless and less suited to village life. His solitary nature rebelled at constant camaraderie, although he enjoyed the goodwill and good humor of the Arapaho community. Whenever Isabella was free, they rode together through the high grasses under the immense sky. They enjoyed their privacy together. Barnabas admired Isabella in the deeply fringed deerskin dress her widowed friends had made for her. She wore her slouch hat with the emerald hatpin holding it fast against the wind. While Ramon healed, she borrowed Segundo. Her handsome El Caballo Valiente, once known as Macaroni, and the unforgiving Little Bay did not rub along well. When they brushed against each other, they squealed and nipped and kicked.

"Perhaps I was too hasty in claiming Valiente for myself," she sometimes admitted to Barnabas. "But he is so very pretty. Not kind, however." And she would stroke his glossy arching neck in sweet regret for his bad nature. As Ramon healed to the point where he had mastery over the fractious chestnut, she was happy to swap mounts and ride the plain but reliable Segundo.

She chatted gaily about her apprenticeship with the four widows. She was learning the intricacies of sewing and ornamenting deerskin, showing off her work with quills and tiny cowrie shells and glass beads on the dress and moccasins she wore. She was excited by the beautiful traditional patterns, applying them with the fine stitching she had learned in her convent. Barnabas said little but listened attentively. He recognized that Isabella would not be long content there among the widows. While she and her brother found safe refuge on these open plains, she was biding her time.

"I promised to escort you to Santa Fe, Isabella. When you judge the time is right, we go. You will be happy back among your people."

"I am happy now, Barny. But where will you go? Where will home be for you?"

"Into that," he replied, pointing to the mountains to the west. "Into Ute country and beyond with Squando."

"Ramon is possessed with a craze for gold. He grew up on tales of Spanish conquistadores seeking vast wealth in the mountains of the north. Now, he is on their doorstep with freedom to come and go as he pleases. He left early this morning on Valiente to hunt for gold, not for game. I fear he believes he will discover a vein of gold that will make him wealthy beyond measure. This has always been Ramon's weakness. Wealth without work."

Isabella was right in her concern. Ramon had learned the trick of following watercourses, looking for the glint of gold in the gravel of their shallows. He often lost all sense of time and distance in his search. The Arapaho spoke of gold dismissively. They knew it was a dangerous lure for white people.

But everyone liked young Ramon, and sometimes other young people would ride out with him. Eventually, they found it boring to search for gold instead of antelope. No one was riding with Ramon today, and when Isabella and Barnabas returned to the village late that afternoon, he had not returned. Valiente, however, had.

Young boys herding horses saw the riderless chestnut galloping home. They marked the direction from which he had come—west from the slopes of the Mountain of the Sun. After a chase, they caught the wayward chestnut. While two of the boys took him back to the village, two older boys rode their ponies in search of Ramon, expecting to find him limping back on foot. There was no sign of the Spanish youth, but they did find a pattern of alarming tracks. Other Indian ponies had passed this way. They debated whether to lie low and wait for the search party to catch up or to go in rescue of their Spanish friend. They made the wrong choice.

In the village, the Raven heard the excited report of the two boys bringing in Valiente. He looked the horse over carefully, seeing no trace of blood but pulling distinctive thistles from his mane and tail. The horse had come through high thistles that grew along a low creek bed in the foothills of the Mountain of the Sun. He knew the location well from childhood when youngsters were sent to harvest the thistles for their seeds. He also knew that the white man's golden devil gleamed in that creek bed.

By the time Barnabas and Isabella returned, the Raven had already dispatched Squando and Two Rivers to look for both Ramon and the two boys who had not reported back to the village. Alarmed, Barnabas immediately saddled Patrick with Little Bay's tack and cinched a saddle pad over Henry. He needed a fresh horse beneath him and a mount for Ramon. He had trouble dissuading Isabella from riding with him and set off in pursuit, leaving her standing forlornly behind.

Squando and Two Rivers had marked their trail with the wooden stakes wrapped in the faded red cloth of Isabella's discarded skirt. They knew that Barnabas would be riding fast behind them as soon as he heard that Ramon was in danger. The stakes confirmed for Barnabas that he was traveling in the right direction as darkness began to fall. He came upon his friends in the last of the light. They had not seen the two boys but had been tracking them west.

The tracks led up a dry canyon, narrowing the higher into it they rode. Their ears strained for any telltale sound, their eyes for campfire light. Darkness made the canyon impenetrable. There were no magical Indian eyes to see by nor the light of stars. They made a dark camp and waited for first light.

Two Rivers assured them that this canyon opened into a high valley. Through this pass, peoples of the plains crossed into the mountain territory of the Utes. The Utes traded beaver pelts and flint for buffalo hides and pemmican with the Arapaho. This traditional trade alliance had diminished with the advent of the Spanish with their horses and the French with their guns, but relations remained amicable.

In the early light of day, chilled to the bone, they climbed higher out of the canyon walls into a high valley watered with a creek lined with trees. Smoke rose from a small circle of tipis. Hobbled ponies grazed in the dew-silvered meadow grass. The trio of riders paused on a low ridge, looking down into a Ute hunting camp. A band of mounted warriors rode out to challenge the trespassers. Two Rivers had his story ready and greeted them in passable Ute. "We ride in peace to bring home two boys who have strayed from Arapaho country in search of a mad young Spaniard. He is under the protection of our clan chief, Young Raven."

"Young Raven still lives?" questioned a surprised older Ute huntsman. Two Rivers knew him by his reputation.

"He has returned from a vision quest on the banks of the Great River, Walking Man. With him, he brought this man, the renowned Abenaki Prophet Squando," and Two Rivers pointed sweepingly to Squando, who lifted his hand in greeting. "The young Spaniard and his sister and this veteran of the Eastern Wars, who is an adopted brother to the Abenaki Prophet, are guests of Young Raven. You will see that both these warriors have been initiated into the Red Circle cohort of the Arapaho." Squando and Barnabas dutifully pulled back their vests to expose the still raw insignia of their new rank. Two Rivers, a born diplomat, cannily elaborated on all the credentials of those seeking Ramon and the boys.

Walking Man was suitably impressed. His party was fixed on an early fall hunt to stockpile for the winter, and they had no special interest in the two Arapaho boys. Boys were always going astray despite the strict discipline of their elders. It was the nature of boys. The young Spaniard presented a problem. He had been found with a pouch full of gold nuggets and resisted angrily when it was wrested from him.

The Ute chose to honor the traditions of hospitality. The visitors at their camp had come in peace on a legitimate errand. He invited them to their cooking fires before the negotiation. Two of his men returned from a reconnaissance to report quietly in his ear that the trespassers were alone.

In the camp, the two Arapaho boys bounded forward in good spirits, relieved to see their kinsman, Two Rivers. They knew they had incurred punishment, but that could wait for the judgment of their seniors. Everyone ate from the camp pots, the women scooping up gourds full of savory stew. Eventually, Ramon was escorted from one of the tipis, hobbled as a sign of captivity. The gold nuggets weighed heavily against him. He had robbed the Ute and endangered their territorial boundaries. Ramon himself was unconvinced of his peril. He swaggered and greeted his rescuers with an airy "Hola, amigos."

Walking Man produced the damning evidence against Ramon and threw open the pouch of nuggets at his feet. Despite the hobble, Ramon sprang forward, scrabbling in the dirt to retrieve his treasure. "My gold," he shouted defiantly at Barnabas, "I found it, and I'm keeping it. Isabella will see that I am the man of my family." When Walking Man contemptuously kicked away the nuggets, the youth sobbed in frustration. Ramon made a sorry spectacle of himself.

"What do you see for the future of the Utes, Prophet?" Walking Man demanded of Squando. "Will white men like this one come in search of gold, and then will more come after them? Our healers know of no cure for this madness."

Squando regarded Ramon, mumbling on the ground with unease. The youth was his sworn friend, not to be left behind. This was not the time to share his visions. "I propose a plan," he suggested through hand talk and Two Rivers as translator. "Let these young men go back to their people, and I will stay and tell your elders the visions I have seen. If they kill me, perhaps they kill the prophecy. Without gold to show, this young man is only another crazed white man dreaming of riches that don't exist. He will be taken to Santa Fe in the south and put in the care of holy men. They can cure him with holy words and holy water."

Walking Man considered the proposition. He was a lesser chief and did not have the authority to judge its merits. He did not believe in the power of the white holy men, but he did believe in the sincerity of the Abenaki Prophet. His elders would value his words. He did not regard the young Spaniard alone as a genuine threat but as an example of how a dropped guard could imperil his people. He knew that waves of native peoples, like this young Abenaki Prophet, had fled the wars and land thefts of the white men to the east of the Great River. Indians came for new lands. Competition would be fierce. But white men would come for gold. They would desecrate the sacred earth.

Barnabas went to his unhappy friend and extended his hand to lift him from the ground. He could not return to Isabella without her brother. One defense of the young man occurred to him, and he took hold of Ramon's legging to bare his tattooed thigh. With a dramatic flourish, he turned

Ramon to show off the raw circles painted blue in the Arapaho tradition.

"Look here," he signed in hand talk mixed with French, "the marks of a warrior wounded by Kiowa. See the tattoo of the Arapaho. Young Raven considers him a son." It was something more for Walking Man to consider. To offend the ancient Arapaho military hero, who returned from a great distance on a vision quest, was an offense against all the elders.

"Go to our chiefs, Squando the Abenaki," Walking Man urged him, "and tell them your prophecies. This young man is free to return to Young Raven without our stolen property. He would be wise to return to his people before we catch him again in our territory. He must pay with his life if we do."

Barnabas offered Squando his Jaeger rifle as a gift to present in goodwill to the Ute chiefs he would encounter. It was all he had with him of value, but he made the sacrifice willingly for the sake of Squando's safe return.

Squando smiled but shook his head, "No, Barny, any gifts must come from me. This pistol of the dead lieutenant will serve that purpose. I never put much faith in either his British horse or his British gun."

"Squando, we are brothers. The Great Spirit has given you a vision quest that you honor wherever you go. I want to honor it with you. First, I must honor our pledge to our Spanish friends to return them to their family. But I will find you and join you. People who hear you will see through your eyes the danger of the white man to the way of the buffalo. We will show what an Abenaki and a man from Vermont can do in alliance." It was a lot of words from the taciturn Barnabas Locke.

EIGHT

THE PLACE OF THE RED WILLOWS

"We go now!" and Isabella stamped her foot emphatically. "He can't be trusted!"

Barnabas agreed. But his heart was sore at leaving Squando behind, somewhere beyond the Mountain of the Sun. The Raven, the elders, and the affectionate widows saw the danger in Ramon's pursuit of gold. The Red Circle cohort offered to accompany them to the border with the Pueblo peoples. From there, the trio would travel the rough track called the Santa Fe Trail, south through Taos and into Santa Fe. They would likely encounter Spanish traders and soldiers traveling the same trail north. Ramon had gone quiet, whether from repentance or resentment was unclear even to Isabella.

She mourned leaving her apprenticeship with her widows and their easy camaraderie, laughing over their work together. She would miss the flirtatious rides with Barnabas, who remained a mystery she had not quite solved. She felt pulled out of this happy dream back into the proper life of a Spanish señorita, responsible for her younger brother and the family name.

The party of three packed their belongings. Isabella rummaged in her canvas bag and pulled out the blue dress folded neatly on the bottom. It would do for Santa Fe. She put it back, along with the embroidered purse clinking with gemstones, her father's pistol, and the purloined bracelet. She added samples of her beaded and quilled leather-work—a belt, a hatband, bridle ornaments, and a few small pouches to give as presents when she saw her family again. She put the finishing touches to a pair of men's moccasins intended for Barnabas as a parting gift.

Ramon had only a short stack of pelts to show for his summer on the plains. Among them, he hid the few gold nuggets he had salvaged. He had a reliable black horse, Segundo. Isabella was welcome to the flashy but faithless Valiente, who had abandoned him.

Barnabas packed his share of the summer's take of pelts and hides and a buffalo robe for each of them onto Patrick and Henry, fat from the long summer graze. He swapped the last of his trade goods for foodstuffs for himself and his string, two horns of powder from the Red Circle keg, and two bars of lead for making round balls for the Jaeger and his German pistol. He sharpened his tomahawk, cleaned and primed his weapons, checked and repaired Little Bay's tack, shook out the saddle blankets and freshened his bedroll with sweetgrass.

The Raven kept Squando's cache for his return. His lodge felt sadly emptied of the vitality and youth of his guests. They had left him well provisioned for the onslaught of winter, but the Raven was content that this happy summer was likely his last.

The morning they left was sharp with the bite of fall. If luck traveled with them, they would arrive in Santa Fe before the early snows. With Two Rivers and two others from the Red Circle, the little party turned south through the yellowing tallgrass, keeping the looming mountains on their right. The same flocks they had watched in the spring migrating north now accompanied them on their southern journey. They traveled easily for several days, each of them secretly hoping Squando would gallop up behind them on Fearless, his plain brown horse. But Squando did not appear. On the morning of the fifth day, Two Rivers signaled a stop in the shade of cottonwoods bending over a stream. They had arrived at the southern border of Arapaho lands. The Pueblo peoples—the Taos, the Nambí, the Acoma, and the warlike Diné—all claimed territory from this point southward. So, too, had the Spanish with their Christian God for nearly two hundred years.

"Barnabas, you are always welcome in our lodges. You are a brother of the Red Circle forever. We will watch for Squando, our brother and prophet." Two Rivers plucked an eagle feather from his head and passed it to Ramon. "Never forget that you wear on your leg the tattoo of your Arapaho family. Keep our secrets; wear your honor as proudly as this feather in your hair."

To Isabella, he said, "Farewell, little sister. You have been like sweetgrass in our village." With those final words, their escort parted from them. No one looked back.

The landscape altered with the miles. They traveled upward as the plains fell behind. The days grew shorter and the nights chillier. They unpacked the buffalo robes and wrapped up in them, sitting close to the campfire. Cottonwoods towered over the shallow waterways. Juniper, scrub oak, and an occasional outcropping of red sandstone dotted the hillsides. The freely trotting Henry learned a painful lesson. Thorny plants were neither edible nor safe to brush against. Isabella patiently picked the spines from his neck.

Barnabas suggested they prepare their story for the inevitable encounter with Spanish soldiers on patrol. Ramon spoke up abruptly, "The truth, no stories. Isabella and I represent the Casa de Flores of Mexico City. We need offer no explanation other than that we have traveled from St. Louis overland on this Santa Fe Trail, with the blessing of Father Bernard. You, Barny, serve as our guide and hunter."

Barnabas asked pointedly, "And how do you explain, Señor Flores, that you and your respectable sister wear Indian clothes?"

"Would you have us naked in the wilderness? Naturally, we have adopted suitable attire to disguise ourselves among the savages. We stayed briefly among the Arapaho while I recovered from a Kiowa arrow. That is our truth." Barnabas caught the tone of assertion in Ramon's voice. "Hah," he thought, "the Spaniard emerges."

Isabella gently interceded. "Yes, Ramon, we have no reason to hide our true identities. However, we must first ascertain that Joe Fontaine has not traced Diego and Della Ramirez to Santa Fe. We should send a message ahead to Fray Atanasio Dominguez, who expects us. Once we are safely under his protection in Santa Fe, we can send word to our uncle that we have passed safely through the wilderness and expect an escort on our way home to the family."

Barnabas read the hard, dry earth for the subtle signs that they traveled the trail to Santa Fe. Previous travelers had left helpful pointers—a broken arrow pointing from an elk skull, mounds of flat stones, wide scrapings of bark marking tall trees. They climbed and dropped again and again through passes, always in the shadow of towering snow-capped peaks. The harsh terrain seemed to heave and buckle and cascade in wide panoramas. Groves of aspens showered them with golden leaves. In the nights, they listened to the chorus of howling wolves and sometimes the scream of a puma. The horses struggled on the upward treks, their riders dismounting to give them a breather. Valiente lost his high step and the proud arch of his neck. The air smelled of snow. Barnabas was the first to spot small bands of Indians herding their sheep out of the hills to lower winter pastures. Gradually, the trail became wider, and the trio, travel-worn and unwashed, approached with grateful relief the place of the red willows, the ancient Pueblo village of Taos nestled in the foothills.

Before they could enter the dried mud walls, a Spanish cavalry patrol, bayonets and silver mountings flashing in the sun intercepted them. The captain, a darkly handsome man with angry eyes and a scar deep across one cheek, accosted them.

"Are you aware," he demanded as though by practiced rote, "that by the Alcalde's decree, all traders who trespass into Nuevo Mexico will be apprehended, taken to Santa Fe for interrogation, relieved there of their possessions, and most likely their liberty. The sale of horses and guns to settlers and Indians," and here he looked pointedly at heavily laden Patrick and Henry, "is strictly forbidden."

Ramon leaped in before Isabella could utter a word in their defense. "We are not 'traders,' Señor Capitan, and we have not 'trespassed' into the precincts of Santa Fe. You see before you Ramon Ignacio Flores and his sister, the Señorita Isabella Blanca Flores. We have the honor to be the nephew and niece of the esteemed merchant of Mexico City, Don Juan Alvarez Flores of the Casa de Flores. We return, after many dangers and vicissitudes, via Santa Fe to our family home."

"You look no more than a pair of renegade whites. Look at that feather in your hair, young man! And this one," the Spaniard sneered at Barnabas, "is most likely a rogue with a fancy long rifle and horses packed with trade goods. Did I not say 'no horses, no guns'?"

Barnabas caught the gist of this sharp exchange. He had picked up some useful Spanish during his long, lazy rides with Isabella. But he held his tongue. Ramon did not. He retorted in icy tones.

"May I introduce Mister Barnabas Locke, a veteran of the War in the American colonies—our allies, as you will please remember, against the British. Locke serves in my employ as a guide, a bodyguard for my sister, and a hunter to sustain us on our rigorous journey to Santa Fe from St. Louis."

Isabella spoke up sweetly but firmly. "Capitan, I have with me a letter of introduction written and signed some months ago in St. Louis by Father Bernard. It is addressed to Fray Atanasio Dominguez of the Mission de San Miguel. Surely you know him? Will you kindly do me the favor of sending a messenger to Fray Atanasio so that we may be welcomed into Santa Fe properly attired?" Isabella smiled her most winning smile. She lifted one languid hand to her hat, removed the emerald hatpin, and doffed the disreputable thing to the captain with a bow from her seat on Valiente. She knew exactly how fetching she looked, even in her rumpled Indian dress.

Somewhat mollified, the Spanish captain introduced himself. "I am Capitan Inigo Antonio Martinez at your service." He returned Isabella's salute with a deeper bow and doffed his cockade with its red badge to her.

The captain unbent so far as to dispatch a young courier on a fast horse to the Mission de San Miguel to confirm that the Flores brother and sister were expected. Further, he permitted the weary travelers a night's lodging within the mission house. Isabella summoned Indian women to prepare a hot bath and to shake out the creases from her blue dress. Clean and refreshed, she donned the blue dress and slipped around her wrist the wide, silver bracelet she had taken from Joe Fontaine's locked chest. She and her brother, although not Barnabas, were invited to join the captain at dinner. After washing up under a cold pump, Ramon borrowed suitable clothes from a like-sized lieutenant. As natural as breathing, the brother and sister set about charming their host. They drank wine and ate with forks and chatted volubly in Spanish about recent adventures.

Captain Martinez assigned three soldiers to accompany him as escort. Two days and more of hard riding lay between Taos Pueblo and Santa Fe. The woman might slow them down, as might the American's pack horses, and there was always the threat of ambush by a Comanche raiding party. He fingered the Jaeger rifle he had appropriated from the quiet young frontiersman. They set off at first light. If the friar was at the mission to meet with the courier, then his man must encounter them on his return.

Barnabas watched Isabella flirt with the captain and wondered if this was how she had ensnared Joe Fontaine. She was ever a puzzle to him. He noted that, although she had resumed her Indian dress and rode astride, she also wore the silver bracelet on her sun-browned arm.

"We will find you a proper sidesaddle, Señorita. Santa Fe may be small, but we have shops on the plaza for our ladies and a good saddlery. And to you, Ramon, I will give the address of my tailor.

Señorita, you will be enchanted by the jewelry makers who squat under the Portal. Perhaps that silver bangle on your lovely arm was fashioned by one of our Pueblo people."

The captain was inclined to be expansive, and although he seemed to ignore Barnabas, he was aware of the hard-eyed, alert young man riding the sturdy bay behind him. They paused only briefly during daylight to rest the horses and rode into the last of the light before making camp. They ate cold meat, hard cheese and harder bread, washed down with a slightly sour wine. The detainees wrapped up gratefully in their warm buffalo robes as the night sky blazed with stars and a rounding moon made sharp shadows on the hard ground. It was late on the second day before the courier on a fresh horse met them on the trail. The captain rode forth to hear his report privately. The news darkened his scarred face, and he cast a suspicious look over his shoulder. He retained the courier under his command as another pair of eyes and rejoined the escort, still reading the message handed to him.

"You are not expected in Santa Fe, Señor, Señorita. The Flores name is not known there. Fray Atanasio acknowledges that he knows Father Bernard, but he has not heard from any uncle in Mexico City. Your tío was to make arrangements for your arrival in Santa Fe, was he not? Did I misunderstand?" The captain refolded the paper in his hand and tucked it into his red sash. "However, there is an American in Santa Fe looking for his Spanish wife and her brother. Their names are Della and Diego Ramirez. They travel in the company of a young American and an Indian. You talked of sheltering with Indians. Is this not odd?"

Barnabas followed the thread of the captain's remarks by the string of names. Those of Diego and Della Ramirez alarmed him. They sent a tremor through Isabella, who cried out, "Joe Fontaine. He is not my husband. He is a river pirate. He murdered our Father." Ramon erupted into a volley of angry words too swift for Barnabas to decipher. Things had suddenly gone very wrong.

Isabella flourished the letter of introduction signed by Father Bernard in the face of Captain Martinez. "Here is proof of our true identity. In it, Father Bernard writes that he will send word to our Tío Juan. That letter must have been intercepted by Joe Fontaine. Oh, that villain! How else could he have traced us to Santa Fe?" She was in a state of fearful excitement.

The captain took the letter from Isabella's trembling hand. He read it over carefully and then again before handing it back. He was unconvinced, but his courier had also reported an odd coincidence at the Mission. Fray Atanasio had scribbled the account and given it to the courier to put into his captain's hands. He wrote that he was surprised by the courier's message from the Flores brother and sister, of whom he had never heard. Yet, only the day before he had heard a description that matched them in every particular, including their hired man. Only the name given was Ramirez. This description was being spread by a large American man called Señor Fontaine, who offered a reward for information as to the whereabouts of his young Spanish wife and her brother. He traveled with rough men, the friar added in a hasty postscript, including several mercenaries of mixed Comanche blood. The courier confirmed that he had himself glimpsed a band of men hastily mounting horses in the plaza as he rode through. The captain kept this ominous incident to himself, saying only in a grave voice, "This matter must go before the Alcalde." He also kept private that the courier believed he had been followed.

NINE

THE OUTPOST

Barnabas rode Little Bay forward to the captain's side. It annoyed him that he had to look up into that arrogant Spaniard's face on his tall horse. He broke his silence. He suspected Captain Martinez spoke better English than he spoke Spanish. Between them, with a smattering of French, they made themselves understood.

"You know that I served in the war. I was a courier and scout, much like your own man. One instinct we couriers share is we can smell an ambush waiting. I smell an ambush. I have already fought this man Joe Fontaine on the banks of the Mississippi. Señorita Flores walloped him over the head with a barge pole and saved my life. She was never his woman."

The captain understood him well. "I share the same instinct. Take back your fine rifle. It's too heavy anyway. I think perhaps you are a very good shot." The two men, disliking one another, became allies in the face of danger.

They rode hard into the waning daylight. The captain had no hope of reaching Santa Fe before nightfall but aimed instead for an abandoned adobe outpost that, in years past, had served as a warning station against Comanche raiding parties. The outpost stood close to the trail and was watered by a small spring-fed stream flowing under low willows. Travelers still sought shelter there and kept the corral in rough repair. Strategically, the post had been built partly under a rock ledge—a good place to post a sentry through the coming night. The captain sent his courier ahead to make sure the outpost was empty.

The trail dropped. Sharp eyes scanned the brushy hillsides around them for a telltale flash or a tumbling stone. It was the pack horse Patrick, always alert to danger, who reared up his head and whinnied the alarm. At once, Barnabas called out, "We're under attack!" and kicked Little Bay beside Isabella on Valiente. "Drop down on his neck and follow me close."

The soldier posted at the head of the column fell dead in a heap from his horse, an arrow through his throat. The captain immediately launched his column into a dead run towards the outpost. From the hillside above came a spattering of arrows, most falling short as the column below veered off the trail into the station clearing.

At the outpost, the courier had quickly reset fallen rails at the corral and held up the sagging gate as the ragged column rode in. Behind them galloped the riderless cavalry mount of the dead soldier. The captain ordered each of his three men to take cover, posting one man on the ledge above as a pair of eyes on the facing hill. Ramon and Isabella hurriedly unlashed supplies from the horses and carried them into the dust and debris of the station. Isabella retrieved her father's pistol from her canvas bag. Ramon seized the rifle still strapped to the fallen soldier's saddle. It held one precious ball; the soldier must have carried his cartridges on his person. The captain stationed himself within the post to cover the empty windows and door. Barnabas went in rapid search through the saddlebags for his confiscated pistol and tomahawk, cursing their absence. Suddenly, the captain was at his shoulder and, smiling thinly, handed over the weapons to their owner.

"If we survive, it may be because of these weapons in my hand," Barnabas said with cold conviction.

Night falls fast and cold in the mountains. In a few hours, the moon would rise, a full autumn moon, casting a silvery light of half-day in this thin, high air. The dark would hide in the shadows. Even as the sun dropped, the bright light of fires flared on the hillside opposite. Joe Fontaine's voice boomed into the night. It echoed among the stony hills.

"Did I not tell you, Della, that I would find you? You ran, and yet here I am. Give me what's mine, and your brother will live. Maybe these soldiers will live too if they play their cards right." The pirate laughed uproariously as though at a fine joke.

Captain Martinez grasped the situation with a military mind. He called up to the soldier flat on his belly on the ledge above. "How many?" A quiet voice answered him. "I see movement but can't tell how many at each fire. They seem spread out among four camps on the hillside across the trail."

Barnabas spoke. "We used this ploy in battle. One side pretends to have more soldiers than they have by lighting scattered fires. But it takes only two men to keep a fire going. One man looks for wood to feed it. One man keeps it blazing. When the fires die down, the men are on the move." Martinez nodded impatiently. "Comanches do the same. We know our enemies."

Joe Fontaine persisted loudly from his fire, careful not to expose his bulky silhouette to Locke's deadly rifle. "Della, get yourself out here. And bring me that fat ruby! Likely that ruby has got a bagful of playmates."

Isabella jerked forward. The captain patted her arm. "It's all a bluff," he said. "They need to take you in the night. The Alcalde is expecting our arrival even now. Tomorrow morning, he will dispatch a patrol." The captain disguised his doubt of an early rescue. The Alcalde was a man seldom in a hurry.

The captain went to each of his posted soldiers with canteens, throwing one up to the lookout on the ledge. "Drink sparingly. No light or noise or sudden movement. Keep low. If something moves within range, kill it."

Fire is always the best weapon in a dry country. As the full moon rose and shed its light impartially, the attackers kept up an unnerving assault of flaming arrows. Most thudded harmlessly against the adobe walls, and a few penetrated through gaping windows. Isabella quickly smothered those with a buffalo hide. After each arrow attack, Joe Fontaine taunted his prey. "I'm coming for you, Della. Send her out, fellows, and Joe Fontaine rides away happy." His boisterous laughter was more irritating than his threats.

Nerves break, or a tired man gets careless. Several shots rang out in quick succession. The unlucky lookout cried out and tumbled into the corral below. His comrade on the left flank rose unwisely from behind his broken wall and responded. The flashpan and muzzle blast exposed his position. Two shots came in return, and at least one found its mark. Barnabas knew this tactic. He reflexively raised his Jaeger and fired into the exact spot revealed by the second musket round, then dropped flat. He was rewarded by the clatter of a gun bouncing down the stony hillside. Tight to the ground, he crawled behind the outpost to safely reload his long rifle. He found Ramon trapped inside the corral, trying to pull out the fallen body of the sentry and the unfired musket that had fallen with him.

Squealing horses milled about, bumping against the flimsy railings. They were not as terrified by smoking arrows or by volleys of gunfire as by the dead man fallen into their midst. Barnabas ducked into the corral to help Ramon drag the dead soldier to the back wall. As the horses settled, he ducked again between rails to retrieve the musket, its bayonet glinting in the moonlight. He handed it to Ramon, who was searching the lookout's body for his cartridge pouch in the dark shadow cast by the back wall. Ramon was now armed with two muskets but only a few round ball cartridges.

An uneasy hush fell. Even Joe Fontaine went quiet, likely plotting a new tactic. Barnabas took the moment to find Little Bay huddled in a corner of the corral. He put his arms around the kind head and stroked his nose until Little Bay lipped his hand for the expected treat. Barnabas heard Ramon calming Valiente with a soothing string of Spanish compliments. He noted with a dry inner laugh that it was not the reliable Segundo who merited Ramon's attention.

Barnabas left the corral and crawled through the back window into the outpost to report. He handed over the second of the muskets Ramon had collected. He reported that the musket of the third dead soldier had fallen on the other side of the broken wall, too exposed by moonlight to retrieve. The captain was incensed. Three of his soldiers had been picked off, two within as many minutes. Only he and the young courier remained of his command. He was now armed with two loaded muskets, his pistol and his sword; the courier with his musket and pistol. Locke had his weapons. Ramon was armed with the musket the youth had taken from the saddled horse. He discounted the woman.

Barnabas also had been counting. Trained by Indian masters of warfare by stealth, Barnabas presented the captain with a plan, a desperate one, but sometimes those succeed through sheer audacity. "We got a dead soldier behind this wall. We got ten horses. We put the soldier on a horse and send him to Santa Fe for reinforcements. Say we release three other horses at the same time. All those horses galloping towards Santa Fe will trigger pursuit from Joe Fontaine. He will surely send men after them. And if even one of the decoys gets through…." Barnabas shrugged.

Joe Fontaine's raucous good humor had darkened into ugly threats. Barnabas and the courier clambered through the back window, leaving the captain to protect the front approach. Behind the wall, Barnabas spoke urgently with Ramon about his sister. He confided the second part of his plan that he had withheld from Captain Martinez.

The three young men lifted the dead soldier and strapped his inert body upright in the saddle of one of the calvary mounts. The horse exhibited military discipline. The captain came to the window to hand through the note from Fray Atanasio, and Barnabas stuffed it into the dead soldier's breast pocket as a message to the living.

Unbuckling the reins and bits from the bridles, they chose the calvary horses as most likely to return to familiar stables in Santa Fe. Ramon and the courier each led two of the decoy horses to the corral gate. Barnabas held the gate open as they lashed the horses through, setting them on the trail to Santa Fe. The sudden thunder of many hooves reverberated among the hills. As the drumbeat diminished, another set of two horsemen went in pursuit. This part of the plan had tricked Joe Fontaine into the loss of men he could ill spare. Barnabas slipped into the darkness to execute the second part of his plan.

TEN

BLOOD UNDER
THE MOON

Barnabas carried his tomahawk in his belt over his right hip, and his pistol tucked crossways on his left hip. Stock to his shoulder, he held the Jaeger rifle at the ready as he stealthily approached the first of the four fires. Only one man alive tossed the last of a pile of juniper branches onto the flames. Nearby, a body lay under a blanket. As the ruffian gazed thoughtfully into the fire, Barnabas smashed the heavy butt of the Jaeger against his neck, snapping the spinal cord. The man fell silently into the flames, igniting a small shower of embers. Barnabas was already gone.

At the second campfire, he found two men alighting arrows for another barrage into the outpost. One notched a crude arrow to his bow, raised it and glimpsed in that instant the flash of a tomahawk whirling past him. He swung his bow towards the figure emerging from the dark and fell face forward with a bullet hole in his forehead. Barnabas yanked his tomahawk from the back of the man at the fire and calmly paused to reload the Jaeger. Before the boom from the shot had stopped reverberating, he was gone from the second campfire.

The fire at the third camp was dying, although a pile of branches lay alongside. Barnabas, in deep shadow, waited motionless for a long moment. A row of picketed horses stamped and swiveled questioning ears in his direction. No man tended either the fire or the horses. In his mind, Barnabas recreated two riders hastily mounting and riding hell-bent after the decoy horses burst from the outpost. He counted eight saddled horses on the picket line.

Barnabas half-slid down the hillside to the fourth campfire. The element of surprise had been lost, but he was still counting in his head. He had dispatched four men and decoyed two more away. As the three men below him turned their faces and weapons upward, he recognized the large man with the sword. The odds were against him. Skittering to a stop, he aimed his rifle at the bulk of Joe Fontaine. As he pulled the trigger, his worn moccasin slid in the loose shale, and the shot struck not the large man but the sword from his hand. It flashed in an arc above the campfire. Two musket balls singed the air by his ears.

"Aha," the big man shouted, "you missed. Now, what will you do, woman stealer?" Barnabas dodged into a thicket of junipers and was lost in the shadows. As he leaped from cover to cover, he shouted back, "I've evened the odds, Joe Fontaine. We're coming for you! You'll be dead before morning." But in his head niggled a horse count and a man count that did not match by one.

He made it by the skin of his teeth across the trail and into the clearing. As a drifting cloud obscured the betraying moon, he stooped to retrieve the musket and cartridge pouch of the dead soldier at the broken wall. Inside the smoking outpost, Isabella threw herself against him, sobbing with relief. The captain paced back and forth in a fury. "What the hell were you thinking? You had no orders."

"I did what Americans do. I took the fight to the enemy. Now we outnumber them." He gently disengaged Isabella and handed Captain Martinez the last of the company muskets.

Joe Fontaine was also counting. No one reported from the campfires above. On his orders, two men were chasing horses. The odds had shifted against him. Everything in his nature urged him to attack now, in the moments before the defenders in the outpost could rally. As Isabella had said long ago, Joe Fontaine was a man of "vicious impulse." But he, too, discounted Isabella. He flung his large self into an all-or-nothing attack, leading the charge down the hillside, across the trail and into the clearing, waving his dinged sword in one hand and his pistol in the other. His words thundered into the outpost, "Della, I'm come for you and what you got of mine!"

Captain Martinez, another hot-tempered man with both sword and pistol in hand, stormed from the outpost. Barnabas ordered Ramon to protect Isabella at any cost as he and the courier followed a step behind their captain. The cloud had drifted on, and under the bright gaze of the autumn moon, both the Spaniard and Joe Fontaine, eyes fixed upon one another, brought up their pistols on the run and fired on the same breath. The captain missed his aim, and his ribs were grazed by Fontaine's bullet, spinning him in his tracks. He flung aside his empty pistol, but keeping his feet under him, he met the downward stroke of Joe Fontaine's sword.

Their swords clashed, both men thrusting and parrying ferociously, their breath rasping in the cold mountain air, but the sheer size of Joe Fontaine pressed the wounded captain hard. He staggered, and the pirate bore hotly upon him. Swords and eyes locked together, the captain laughed into the face inches from his own and brought up a strategic knee into Joe Fontaine's groin. As the pirate grunted in pain but still clenched his sword, the captain pressed his bloody hand against Joe Fontaine's chest at arm's length, steadying himself for the final thrust. Standing on the ledge above the outpost, the eighth man fired the clear shot he had waited for into the captain's exposed chest. The captain's sword slipped from his hand as his knees buckled beneath him. With a triumphant shout, Joe Fontaine contemptuously kicked the Spaniard's body into the dirt.

Ramon stepped forward from the empty door-way, an eagle feather in his hair. He brought his musket, fully cocked, to his shoulder, aimed and shot dead the eighth man on the ledge. He scarcely felt Isabella rush past him with their father's pistol steady in her hand. Oblivious to the combat still waging fiercely around her, she confronted the river pirate.

"You are a dead man, Joe Fontaine." She looked him in the eyes with her finger on the trigger. "I kill you with my Father's pistol. It is a just revenge." And she shot Joe Fontaine.

The man laughed even as he hunched yet again in pain. "It's a nice little gun, Della, but I wear a thick leather vest under this coat. It hurts, I give you that, but I ain't dead." He grasped her arm with one hand, his fingers digging the silver bracelet painfully into her skin and her throat with the other. He shook her hard, spitting words into her face, "You're a clever thief, Della Ramirez. You hand over my ruby and that little sack of treasure you picked up in St. Louis. A price to pay for all the trouble you put me through."

As she struggled for breath, Isabella's free hand stopped pounding Joe Fontaine's wounded chest and went instead to pluck the emerald hatpin from her head. The slouch hat fell at her feet as she stabbed her mother's pin deep into the wrist gripping her throat. Joe Fontaine yelled in outrage. This damn woman was besting him yet again.

With that, his eyes widened in surprise, his hands loosened their grip, and blood trickled from his mouth. The large body swayed, and as Isabella stepped aside, Joe Fontaine fell face forward with a tomahawk between his shoulders.

Barnabas grinned wickedly into Isabella's shocked face. He had killed a Comanche mercenary with a pistol shot to the heart as the two locked in a fatal clinch, and in the next breath, he flung his tomahawk twenty paces into the back of Joe Fontaine.

On the other side of the broken wall, the last man standing of Fontaine's gang furiously swung his empty musket against the young courier, who dodged nimbly out of reach. Outweighed and outmatched, the courier kept his head, and using his empty musket with the bayonet attached, he blocked the wild swings. When the last man standing gripped his musket with both hands and raised it above his head, the courier swiftly stepped forward and demonstrated the finer point of a bayonet by thrusting it through his sternum.

ELEVEN

THE COURIER

Although they did not expect the two out-riders to return, they could not leave Isabella unprotected. Ramon and the courier brought in the soldier killed on the trail, the one whose horse was sent with another dead rider to Santa Fe. He joined Captain Martinez and his comrade, who died at the broken wall, in a respectful row under blankets. Joe Fontaine and his three henchmen lay where they died.

The courier found the letter addressed by Father Bernard from St. Louis to Casa de Flores, Mexico City, crumpled inside Fontaine's vest pocket. Other things he kept for himself, but he brought the letter deferentially to Señorita Isabella, waiting in her blue dress on a bale of hides inside the abandoned post. She read the letter aloud to Barnabas as he appreciatively pulled on a pair of new moccasins, strikingly patterned with a design of white quills and colored beads.

"This is all the proof I need of the villainy of that man. Our uncle will ensure that my reputation remains unsullied." She briefly sank into reflection, then roused herself. "Come with me to Santa Fe, Barny. We could make a life there." She smiled, "Ramon will need your guidance."

"Tonight Ramon has shown himself a man, Isabella. I think he needs no advice from me, nor, I believe, do you. We belong to different worlds." The two of them sat together, thinking in companionable silence. Privately, each acknowledged with regret and relief the end of this wonderful adventure with each other.

"Barny, I have a confession to make—not a confession exactly, but an admission. In St. Louis, Father Bernard gave me the gemstones and the Spanish silver and gold my Father left in his safe-keeping. They have been in my canvas bag under this dress all this time. We did trust you. You just didn't need to know."

"I guess I have a sort of confession, too. I never pictured me as a man with a family, with a wife and maybe children. I don't think I have the makings. I would be a disappointment to her and to myself. I don't say I couldn't love them, just not be there for them." Barnabas had never tried to put into words these thoughts. He expressed them awkwardly, but Isabella understood him perfectly. She bent towards him and met his lips with her lips.

A space of time later, Barnabas led the horses one by one from the corral to the stream. The courier and Ramon brought down the eight horses from the hillside. They watered and then picketed them. Barnabas filled his canteens upstream. Ramon helped him strap his goods, including the bale of hides, onto Patrick and Henry. They made private time to say necessary things. Barnabas asked Ramon a favor.

"Would you send a message for me from Santa Fe? To my friend, Joshua Jones, Boat Builder and Land Agent, Cahokia, Illinois Country. Word that I live and am headed north again to meet up with Squando. Mr. Jones will know where to send news of me to my people." They shook hands firmly, and Ramon went to wait with Isabella for the Alcalde's tardy patrol.

At the corral, as Barnabas was cinching Little Bay, the courier approached him and spoke in heavily-accented English. "Señor, before you depart, I wish to properly introduce myself." He bowed. "I am Corporal Ángel Inocente Ruiz. It will be my honor to relay the gallantry of my capitan's death to my superiors. If they permit, I will personally conduct Señorita and Señor Flores into the protection of Fray Atanasio at Mission de San Miguel."

Corporal Ruiz was curious about this man, a scout and courier like himself, admiring his bravery and his quick wits. "Pardon me, Señor, where do you go? I ask because there is a place I want to find someday, and maybe you have been there. A city of the Ancient Ones. They say this city hides in a canyon in the mountains north and west of here. Have you heard of it?" He was an adventurous young man with plans for his future.

Barnabas respected the courier. He reminded him of someone he half-remembered. "Yes, among the Arapaho, stories are told of a forbidden city. I'd like to see it myself. I wish you good luck, Corporal Ruiz. I go north to travel among those tribes, to talk to them with my friend, the Abenaki Prophet Squando. He has important things to say at their councils. I want to know these people and their ways, see the lands they hunt and travel. Perhaps we will find this city of the Ancient Ones. Squando would like that."

The patrol arrived that afternoon. The decoy soldier had fulfilled his duty even in death. The troopers stoically retrieved the bodies of their dead and hastily buried Joe Fontaine and his gang in a shallow ditch, covering the bodies with stones. They confiscated for the government the horses picketed at the stream and for themselves useful things they found. Barnabas Locke on Little Bay, with his pack horses trotting behind, was already miles north on the Santa Fe Trail.

TO BE CONTINUED

About the Author

MATTHEW BLAINE enjoys swapping tales with interesting people with their own stories to tell, especially around a campfire. Although his education was hampered by dyslexia, he found another sort of education in the company of Ernest Hemingway, Jack London, Louis L'Amour, John Steinbeck and outdoors adventure magazines. After stints as a cab driver, steelworker, factory floor assembler, and carpenter, he worked for thirty years managing trade shows on the East Coast. During the pandemic, he wrote two self-printed memoirs about his travel and outdoor adventures. That triggered an ambition to write honest fiction in which he could reinvent himself in the lives of historical characters. An avid primitive archer, canoeist, long-distance hiker, minimalist, and unionist, Matthew enjoys delving into the obscure stories of the past.

Retired, he lives in rural Pennsylvania, haunting flea markets for goods to trade with fellow outdoorsmen at swaps and archery rendezvous. In a shop inside his woods, he practices the skills required for leather working, shaping and fletching primitive arrows, and marrying old axeheads to newly-fashioned handles.

www.ingramcontent.com/pod-product-compliance
Lightning Source LLC
Chambersburg PA
CBHW031844170626
46807CB00004B/1617